Innocent

"What do you want?" Roxanne asked harshly. Vince stood there stiffly, looking terribly serious. "I want to apologize."

Rox stared at him in surprise. "Apologize? You? What are you apologizing for?"

"Roxanne," he said sincerely, "it wasn't right that your name was left out of the newspaper interview. I'm sure they feel really awful about it."

Roxanne's mouth dropped open. Was this guy for real? If he believed what he was saying, he must be even more dense than she'd expected.

Then it dawned on her. Maybe Vince didn't know her history. Maybe he didn't know anything about the Kennedy-Stevenson feud she'd created.

It was all becoming clear now. Vince was a wide-eyed innocent; a babe in the woods.

PLAYING DIRTY

M.E. Cooper

SCHOLASTIC INC.
New York Toronto London Auckland Sydney

ISBN 0-590-41267-1

12 11 10 9 8 7 6 5 4 3 2 1   8 9/8 0 1 2 3/9

Printed in the U.S.A.   01

First Scholastic printing, May 1988

Chapter
1

Just before noon, in the office of Kennedy High's newspaper, *The Red and the Gold*, editor Karen Davis sat on the edge of her desk and surveyed the rapidly filling room. All around her, juniors and seniors were talking excitedly, laughing, and calling to each other. A feeling of giddy exuberance echoed in their conversations. It was June, the sun was shining, and graduation was just around the corner.

On the faces of her friends, Karen could read the mixed emotions they were all feeling. Everyone had term papers to finish, exams to cram for, grades to worry about. But the freedom of summer days on the beach lay just ahead of them, and they were all looking forward to that.

The room was buzzing with anticipation, but there was another feeling, too. For the seniors, it was the end of high school, and many of them were also sad.

A warm feeling surged through Karen as she observed her friends. They were the best crowd in the world. These people were so dear to her. They'd all seen each other through ups and downs, good times and bad. Sure, there'd been times when things hadn't been too terrific. With a shudder, she remembered the bad feelings after the ski trip that winter, when Katie broke her leg and everyone blamed everyone else. For a while, kids weren't even speaking to each other.

In the end, though, they'd pulled together and worked things out. Now they were as close as they'd ever been. And summer would be terrific. The crowd had already staked out a section of the beach where they'd be meeting every weekend for parties and just hanging out.

But then fall would come, and the crowd would split up and leave Rose Hill to go off to various colleges. They'd see each other on holidays and vacations, but it wouldn't be the same. And Karen couldn't help feeling a bit wistful.

"Cheer up," Jonathan Preston said as he ambled by her desk, his fedora cocked at a jaunty angle. "They haven't snatched the editorship away from you yet."

Karen grinned as she looked up at him. "You know, you're right," she said. "I feel better already." She waved to Adam and Elise, two of her reporters.

Jonathan looked out over the crowd. "Big turnout," he commented.

"It should be," Karen said. "This is going to be the biggest issue of *The Red and the Gold* ever. We're doing feature articles on the juniors who are taking our place as leaders next year."

Jonathan flashed her an exaggerated look of dismay. "Gee, and I always thought I was irreplaceable."

"Well, maybe to Lily," Karen said mischievously, with a nod toward the door. Just walking in was a slender, blonde, waiflike girl with a round, impish face.

There was no mistaking Jonathan's happy expression as he immediately turned and headed toward her. Karen smiled and shook her head.

Adam, Elise, and Emily joined Karen at the front of the room a moment later.

"Our last issue," Elise said mournfully.

"It'll be fun doing these interviews, though," Emily commented. "Have you decided who you're going to feature?"

"I'm going to do Josh Ferguson," Elise told her, "He's taking over WKND." She sighed. "I'm going to miss hearing him do that Raspberry Patch show on *Cloaks and Jokes* over the summer. I think it's just charming."

Karen nodded in agreement. Josh Ferguson was a big hit on the school radio station with his program about a mythical town and its downhome inhabitants. "How about you, Emily?"

"Zack McGraw, definitely. With him as captain, the football team's going to be amazing."

"You know, it's funny," Karen mused. "Remember when the Stevenson High kids transferred here at the beginning of the term? The way they acted, I wondered if they'd ever fit in."

"And look at them now," Adam said. "Zack's football captain, Lily Rorshack is taking over the Drama Club. . . ."

"And Frankie Baker is going to be president of the Computer Club," Karen added, smiling and waving at the pale, fair-haired girl who was taking a seat next to Josh Ferguson. "Now that the newspaper article mess is over," she said calmly, recalling the "practical joke" that had been played on her, the newspaper, and WKND, "all the Stevenson transfers are real Kennedy people now." A moment later she saw another girl standing in the doorway and her smile faded.

"I take that back," she amended. "Not *all* the Stevenson transfers."

Roxanne Easton paused in the doorway, her deep green eyes coolly sweeping the room. They were all there — all the leaders, the ruling class of Kennedy High. And not one of them had even said hello to her.

Well, she had a right to be there. After all, hadn't she just volunteered to work on the senior yearbook? Didn't that make her a leader? She would be in charge of all club coverage for the coming year. And if these so-called leaders wanted even the briefest mention of their clubs in the yearbook, they'd better recognize her as an up-and-coming member of the elite herself.

She edged toward a seat in the back, where no one was sitting yet. If nothing else, she could take some comfort in knowing she was the best-looking girl in the room. No wonder the other girls didn't like her, Rox thought. That didn't bother her. In fact, it was to be expected. As for the boys . . . well, she'd made some mistakes, that was for sure.

That thought was confirmed as her eyes met Jonathan's and he immediately looked away. Roxanne sighed. She couldn't believe he was still holding a grudge over that stupid Valentine Day's Dance. So what if she'd made dates with *four* guys? Roxanne liked a little variety. And she'd done a great job buttering them up. But when Jonathan found out she'd been interested in several boys, he'd felt used. Obviously he still hadn't gotten over it, she thought sourly. Well, he was with Lily now. Roxanne had to chalk him up as a lost cause.

She'd made enemies of the other guys, too, but she'd find a way to make them forget. She wasn't finished yet, not by a long shot. And getting a feature story, maybe even her picture, in *The Red and the Gold* was just the beginning.

She slid into her seat, carefully adjusting her pale yellow miniskirt. It looked great against her long, tanned legs. She smoothed back her glossy, tawny red hair and took in the scene around her. Her lips tightened as she noticed the Stevenson kids mingling easily with the Kennedy regulars. Not so long ago, they'd sided with Roxanne and shared her hostility. She had managed to convince them that the Kennedy students were against the Stevenson transfers. She'd had a real feud going for a while. All the Stevenson kids believed that the Kennedy crowd wanted to exclude them, that they would make life at Kennedy as miserable

5

for the transfer students as possible. But now look at them. All her old friends had gone over to the other side — and they'd left Roxanne behind.

Some of the girls even had boyfriends in the crowd. Crazy Lily, Stevenson's former drama star, was involved with Jonathan. And even shy, wimpy Frankie, Rox's ex-best friend, had a boyfriend — Josh Ferguson. Who would have ever thought that dull, mousy Frankie, who used to tag along with Roxanne, who *worshiped* Roxanne, would find herself a boyfriend?

She watched through narrowed eyes as Daniel Tackett paused in front of the room to talk to Karen. Even radical Daniel was brown-nosing . . . starting to break into the crowd! There he was, leaning against Karen's desk, one cowboy-booted foot crossed over the other. He was acting terribly chummy, trying to butter up a girl whose career he'd almost sabotaged just a few months ago.

It was a great scheme, and a small smile played on Roxanne's lips as she remembered it. Daniel had conned Karen into doing an interview with Lily for *The Red and the Gold*. Convinced that no one would get hurt, and that the Kennedy kids deserved a little razzing because they were such elitists, Lily had pulled a real number on Karen, giving her a long sob story about how she had once been a runaway and a hoodlum. And Karen bought the whole thing. She had even been persuaded to submit the interview to a journalism contest!

That's when Frankie had turned traitor and switched sides. When she heard what Lily and

Daniel had done, she got Josh to help her get Karen's entry back before it could be read by the judges. Since then they'd all made up, and everyone was buddy-buddy.

It would have been a great scandal, Roxanne thought regretfully. And there wouldn't be any opportunities like that again. Now all the Stevenson kids had weasled their way into the crowd. She was the only one left to carry on. She, alone, was still on the outs. But not for long, she told herself. She was here as a future leader, one of those about to be honored.

Roxanne sat up straight and fixed her eyes on Karen as the newspaper editor called for everyone's attention. She didn't get it right away.

"C'mon, you guys! I'm calling the meeting to order!"

Finally everyone settled down. Roxanne listened closely as Karen outlined the plans.

"We're devoting the last issue of the newspaper to the juniors who will be leading Kennedy next year. Unfortunately, there isn't going to be enough room to include interviews and pictures of everyone, so I've told the reporters to choose the juniors they want to do an in-depth story on. They're going to tell you now which juniors will get featured. Of course, we'll try to include all the other juniors who are leading school clubs and activities in a general round-up article."

Roxanne's heart sank as she scrutinized the lineup of reporters standing around Karen's desk: Adam, Elise, Emily, Dee. They were all seniors, all members of the crowd. Then she remembered Daniel, and her spirits rose for a moment.

He wasn't in the crowd. But all he wanted to do was to impress Karen, and to do that he pretty much had to pick one of the crowd juniors.

It all went pretty much as Rox expected.

"I'm going to write on Greg Montgomery," Adam announced, and cheers went up from the room for the upcoming student body president. Roxanne cast a bitter glance at the tall, sandy-haired boy. That was the boy she should be with, the one she'd tried hardest to win. And he'd rejected her. Well, he'd be sorry. . . .

The other reporters were announcing their choices. Elise was doing Josh Ferguson, Emily was covering Lily Rorshack and Zack McGraw. Dee went next.

"I'm going to feature Frankie Baker, the next president of the Computer Club."

Roxanne closed her eyes. She couldn't believe what she was hearing. Bland, boring Frankie was getting her picture in a newspaper for running the nerdy Computer Club? Had the world gone crazy?

Uneasily she realized only Daniel was left. Would he choose her? Or was she going to have to settle for some crummy little mention in a general round-up column?

The lanky, long-haired boy stood with his arms folded, his eyes darting around the room. "Is anyone left?" he asked jokingly. "It seems to me all the major big-shots have been chosen."

Josh Ferguson jumped up. "How about Vince?"

Roxanne's mouth dropped open. Vincent Di-Mase? He had to be kidding! Vince was a nobody!

He was an old friend of Josh's, but nobody even knew him!

"Vince is going to be taking over the Wilderness Club," Josh continued enthusiastically. "He'll be leading those nature lovers on their trips. And he's on the volunteer firefighter rescue squad, too."

Roxanne put a hand over her mouth to keep from laughing out loud. *Oh wow*, she thought sarcastically, that's really impressive. He's a nature freak and a macho he-man who probably thinks life's biggest thrill is walking into burning buildings.

She turned slightly to get a long hard look at this paragon of virtue Josh was describing. With his serious expression, dark hair, and broad shoulders, Vince wasn't bad-looking. But his clothes were a dead giveaway. He was wearing hiking boots, worn jeans, a flannel shirt — in June, no less! — and a baseball cap. The king of dorkdom, Roxanne decided.

Surely Daniel wouldn't be interested in doing a feature story on this nobody. But Roxanne's eyes darkened as she saw Karen smiling and nodding with interest as Josh continued to heap praise on his friend. Daniel didn't miss her look, either.

"Sounds good to me," he drawled. "Vince, you're on."

Roxanne sank back in her seat. Cold fury churned inside her. She'd been passed over again. How could they do that to her? She — Roxanne Easton — who should have been queen of the school by now. You fools, she thought angrily.

Do you honestly think you can get away with treating me like that?

The only reason she'd volunteered for that stupid yearbook job was so that she could get a write-up in *The Red and the Gold*. Some help that had turned out to be. Things were definitely not going according to her plan. She was going to have to do some thinking.

The meeting was starting to break up. Roxanne rose quickly, determined to get out of the room as fast as possible.

"Hi, Roxanne," called Frankie, who was standing in front of her. Roxanne started to walk past her without saying anything. She had no use for people who betrayed her. But several people were standing in front of her, and for a minute she couldn't move.

"I heard you signed up to be an editor for the yearbook," Frankie continued. "I'm glad you're getting involved in school activities."

Roxanne looked at her former friend suspiciously. Was there condescension in Frankie's voice? How dare she talk to her like that? But Frankie's face was completely innocent. Her light eyes were reserved but almost friendly.

Roxanne allowed Frankie the briefest possible smile. "I'm going to be the *clubs* editor, you know. That means *I'll* decide what clubs will be featured in the yearbook, and how much space each club gets." And if you think your silly Computer Club's going to get an inch, you're crazy, she added silently. She gave Frankie a meaningful look.

But Frankie just smiled. "That's nice." Then

Josh joined her, tossing an arm casually over her shoulder and not even acknowledging Roxanne's presence.

"C'mon, let's go," he said.

Frankie murmured " 'Bye" to Roxanne, but Roxanne didn't bother to respond. Tossing her head, she whirled around and headed for the door. She'd almost reached it when someone coming from the opposite direction practically walked into her.

Roxanne stepped back, startled. Then she realized who she'd almost crashed into, and a look of contempt crossed her face.

Vince was startled, too, but he recovered quickly. Strangely enough, he didn't seem to read her angry expression at all.

"Excuse me," he said politely. He reached in front of her, opened the door, and then stepped aside so that she could pass through first. For a second, Roxanne was too shocked to move. She stared at him in disbelief.

Vince just stood there, holding the door. His manner was gallant and courtly — almost like he was about to bow to her!

Roxanne rolled her eyes. This gentleman routine wasn't about to impress her. Giving him one brief, cold look, she brushed past him and stormed out into the hallway.

Chapter
2

Lily watched proudly as just about everyone leaving the meeting paused to talk briefly with Jonathan. He was like a magnet, drawing everyone else to him.

Even an alien from another planet would know from looking at Jonathan that he was one of the most popular guys in the senior class. As student activities director, he knew everyone and everyone knew him. Lily wondered if he'd miss all this attention when he graduated. She knew Kennedy High would miss him.

She'd miss him, there was no doubt about that. He was so special to her. Maybe one of the reasons their relationship was going so well was because of the obstacles they'd had to overcome to get together in the first place.

Her thoughts went back to the day she first saw him, in the costume storage room of the Little Theater. She had taken his precious hat and when Jonathan got annoyed and tried to take it back, she'd started doing impersonations of a frantic and impatient Jonathan.

Something had happened in that brief moment — a spark was ignited. But Lily had been convinced they'd never be a couple, spark or no spark. After all, Jonathan's crowd hated the Stevenson transfers, or so Lily had been led to believe.

Roxanne and Daniel certainly seemed to think so. It was Daniel who was responsible for Lily's phony interview with Karen. And when Jonathan found out the trouble that Lily had caused for Karen, he hadn't wanted anything to do with her.

Eventually Jonathan came to realize that Lily had been used and manipulated by Daniel, that she wasn't aware of the part she'd played in creating the Kennedy–Stevenson feud. Finally, after weeks of confusion and misunderstanding, they had worked it all out — just in time for the prom.

The newspaper office emptied rapidly. Practically everyone had left for class. Jonathan was standing in the doorway, talking to Greg, and Karen was straightening up her desk. Lily wandered over to her.

"Don't you have to go to class?" she asked Karen.

Karen shook her head. "I've got journalism, so I'm staying here. What about you?"

"I've got a free period." Lily hopped up and perched herself on a corner of Karen's desk. "I can't believe *The Red and the Gold* is doing a feature story on me." Me, the original Benedict

Arnold, she added silently, still mortified about that interview.

But Karen didn't refer to it. "You're a leader now, so of course there'll be a story on you."

Jonathan ambled over to join them. "Good meeting, Karen. I think it's a great idea, featuring the juniors. It'll introduce them to the rest of the school."

"We're lucky we've got so many interesting juniors to write about," Karen added. "I think we're leaving this school in good hands, don't you?"

Jonathan grinned. "They'd better be good! They've got a big job ahead of them. This isn't exactly an easy joint to run."

Lily laughed. "Thus speaks the King of Kennedy High as he prepares to descend from his throne!" She glanced at the clock. "Hey, don't you have class?"

Jonathan took off his hat and casually pushed his light brown hair out of his eyes. "Yeah, but it's no big deal." He leaned against Karen's desk.

Lily's eyebrows shot up. "No big deal? Mr. Barnes's advanced composition?"

Now Karen looked a little concerned. "In case you've forgotten, Barnes is only the toughest English teacher here. You'd better get a move on, Jonathan. He can't stand for anyone to be late for his class, not even big-shot seniors."

Jonathan brushed Karen's warning aside. "Barnes and me are buddies. He's not going to hold a few minutes against me. What can he do to me, anyway?"

"Flunk you, maybe?" Lily murmured, but Jonathan acted as if he hadn't heard her.

"Hey, did you hear about the skit Molly and Eric worked up for the Senior Follies? It's really wild. It's a takeoff on the Valentine's Day Dance when everyone was matched by computer."

Karen made a face. "Didn't Eric get matched with Roxanne at the dance? As I recall, he didn't find that particularly funny."

Jonathan's eager expression faded. "Yeah, and he wasn't the only one. But we're not doing the skit about *that*. This is supposed to be a comedy, you know. Not a tragedy. Besides, Eric's not going to be in the skit; he just helped Molly write it."

"Is the whole show about the Valentine's Day Dance?" Karen asked him.

"No, just that one skit. The show's going to make fun of all the major events this year. But listen, in Molly's skit, the computer breaks down, and everyone's matched with their complete opposite. It's going to be a riot."

"Have you guys started rehearsals yet?" Lily asked.

"Well, we had one meeting. . . ." Jonathan paused and made a face. "Everyone was horsing around. I'm supposed to be the director, and I couldn't even get them to settle down and listen to me. Not that I actually knew what to tell them. I mean, what do I know about directing, anyway?"

Lily cocked her head thoughtfully. "You don't really know anything about directing. . . ."

"Nothing at all," Jonathan said. He studied

Lily for a moment. "Hey, I've got an idea. You're the drama expert around here. Maybe you could help me with the show."

"But I'm just a junior," Lily objected. "This is the *Senior* Follies, remember? Only seniors are supposed to work on it, right?"

"I don't think that's a *law*," Jonathan said. He turned to Karen. "What do you think? Wouldn't you say Lily's the perfect person to help us put on a really silly, bizarre show?"

Karen nodded in agreement, but Lily pretended to be offended. "Hey, wait a minute. What do you mean, 'the perfect person for a silly, bizarre show?' Are you suggesting that I'm silly and bizarre?"

Jonathan squinted, and he acted as if he were scrutinizing Lily. "No, not silly," he pronounced finally, "and not bizarre, either. Goofy, I guess."

Lily gave him a look of mock astonishment. "Goofy? Me? How dare you?"

Karen was laughing. "I'd say you guys are just about even on the goofiness scale."

"So what do you think?" Jonathan asked, his face and voice back to normal. "It's okay for Lily to help me with the show, right?"

Karen shrugged. "I don't have any problem with it."

"How does that sound to you?" he asked Lily.

"Gee, I'm glad you finally got around to asking," Lily replied. "I'll give it some thought." She placed a hand on her forehead, as if she were concentrating intensely. Then she grinned. "Okay, I'll do it. Hey, it's almost time for the late bell. You'd better dash."

16

"Yeah, in a second," Jonathan said. His relaxed slouch against the desk gave no indication that he had any intention of moving any time soon.

"Well, if you're going to hang around till the last second maybe you could help *me* out," Karen said. "I've got a problem, and I don't know what to do."

Jonathan looked at her with interest. "What kind of a problem?"

Karen's face grew serious. "I don't know what to do about *The Red and the Gold*. I'm supposed to appoint an editor for next year."

"Doesn't the faculty take care of that?" Lily asked.

"Usually," Karen said. "But this year they're going to leave the decision to me, because I'm a better judge of the reporters since I've worked with them more closely."

"Who's in the running?" Jonathan asked.

Karen hesitated. "That's the trouble. I know Daniel Tackett wants it. He's been working like a fiend the past few weeks. I've never seen anyone try so hard to do a good job. He's written articles, he's done research, he's even volunteered to do proofreading, and no one likes doing that. He's been in this office every day during his breaks and after school. Really, it's incredible. One time I came back at night to get a book I left and he was still here, correcting some copy."

"Sounds like he really wants the job," Jonathan said. "Is he qualified?"

"He's probably the most experienced and talented person on the staff," Karen admitted.

"He was the editor of the *Stevenson Sentinel* before he transferred here." She turned to Lily for confirmation, and Lily nodded.

"Then what's the problem?" Jonathan asked.

Karen paused and looked at Lily. Lily sighed, then looked down, and studied the floor. She knew exactly what was troubling Karen.

"I don't know if I can trust him," Karen said at last. "After he got me to print that story about Lily, it's hard for me to believe that he'd have the best interests of the newspaper at heart. He says he's sorry, and he seems sincere, but I don't know. . . ."

"I know the perfect answer," Jonathan said suddenly. "Don't appoint anyone."

Karen looked at him blankly. "Huh?"

"Hang on to the job yourself!" Jonathan grinned. "Look, I know some of the juniors are pretty good, and I suppose a few of them have leadership qualities — "

"Gee, thanks," Lily interjected.

" — but no one's going to do a better job than we've been doing," Jonathan continued. "Let's face it, we're the best senior class this school has ever seen!"

Karen rolled her eyes. "So what are you suggesting, Mr. Bright Ideas? That we just stay here, refuse to graduate, and continue running the school?"

"Not exactly. . . ." Jonathan looked thoughtful. "You know, Charlotte DeVries is supposed to be the next student activities director. Personally, I'm not so sure that's such a great idea."

"Why not?" Lily asked. "You never had any

18

objection to her before now. And she seems like she's qualified."

Jonathan shrugged. "She's a major flirt. And she talks funny."

"That's because she's from the South, you idiot," Karen reminded him. "Besides, what do flirting and having an accent have to do with being student activities director?"

Jonathan laughed and shrugged. "I don't know . . . all I know is I'm holding on to the events calendar."

Karen looked at him in surprise. "You haven't turned it over to Charlotte yet?"

"Nope. Who knows, maybe I'll hang on to the job and run things from U. Penn."

Lily looked at him curiously. He was kidding, of course, but there was something in his voice. . . . Her thoughts were distracted by the ringing of the late bell.

"Jonathan! You're late! Mr. Barnes is going to have a fit!"

Jonathan groaned and picked up the books he'd left on Karen's desk. "I'm really not up for advanced comp today," he muttered.

"Yeah?" Lily retorted. "Well, maybe you're not up for graduating, either."

Jonathan stared at her for a minute. Then his face lit up. "Hey, forget advanced comp. I've got a better idea."

"What's that?" Lily asked suspiciously.

"Its kind of warm in here, don't you think?" Jonathan tipped his hat at a rakish angle over his eyes. "I think I'll go for a swim."

Lily's eyes widened. "A swim? Where?"

19

"In the good ol' JFK pool!" Jonathan's eyes were twinkling, and Lily had a sinking feeling he wasn't making a joke.

"Yeah, that's just what I'm in the mood for," Jonathan continued. "A dip in the pool. And who knows—maybe the freshman girls are having their swimming classes now. I think maybe I'll join them." He sauntered away, pausing at the door to turn back to them.

"Those poor girls aren't gonna know what hit them!" With that, he walked out the door.

Lily stared after him for a minute, and then turned to Karen. Karen was laughing so hard there were tears in her eyes.

"You guys crack me up," she managed to say. "You're perfect together. You're both nuts!"

Lily smiled back at her. But then she turned back toward the door Jonathan had just walked through. Was he serious? Was he really going to cut class to go swimming? Was he making a joke just then? Lily wasn't sure.

Karen was right. They were both goofy, she and Jonathan. And they both liked putting other people on, letting them think they were serious when they weren't.

But this was different. She knew Jonathan, and something in his expression bothered her. He wasn't just kidding around.

Something had suddenly gotten into her boyfriend, and Lily didn't know what it was.

Chapter
3

Katie Crawford sat in the middle row of the bleachers, her eyes fixed on the balance beam. It was the girls' gymnastic finals, and Stacy Morrison was up. Katie watched closely, scrutinizing her every move. Stacy had a tendency to be sloppy. She had enormous potential as a gymnast, but there were times when she didn't work at it hard enough. Katie had been coaching her for the past couple of months, and now she was anxious to see if her work with Stacy was going to pay off.

Her protégée was poised at the foot of the beam. As she went into her mount, Katie sent Stacy silent messages: Focus! Keep your arms up! Straighten that knee!

Stacy executed her mount perfectly, and Katie allowed herself one brief sigh of relief. But she couldn't really relax. She knew too well what was going on in Stacy's head — the intense concentration, the feverish excitement, the fear of failure, the thrill of accomplishment. She'd been there herself not too long ago.

Katie would never be a first-class gymnast again — she knew that. And it was her own fault.

Looking back now, she could see that the ski trip had been a major turning point in her life, in more ways than one. She remembered the jealousy, the intense hostility she had felt on the slopes as the boys flocked around Roxanne, hanging on her every word. Matt, Eric, and Jonathan were practically falling over themselves trying to impress her. And Greg — Katie's Greg — was just as bad as the others, competing for Rox's attention.

Rox was an okay skier, but no expert. So Katie suggested they all try the advanced run, wickedly expecting that Rox just might look really bad on such a steep hill. It was a really rough slope, and as they gathered at the top, even Katie began to have second thoughts. But then Rox had gotten the bright idea that they should race. Katie knew that Rox was just showing off, but there was no way she was going to back out now.

The second they all took off, Katie knew they were in over their heads. Roxanne took a tumble, and Eric tried to rescue her but collided with Katie. In the fall that followed, Katie broke her leg.

Nothing was the same after that. Her leg eventually mended, but she'd never again have the ability to compete seriously in gymnastics. In her anger and despair, she had blamed everyone for the mishap — especially Greg. They went through a wretched breakup, and for a while they couldn't even speak to each other.

At least they'd managed to get beyond that. They were speaking now — in fact, they were actually friends. Katie was at least glad of that. It wasn't like it used to be, but she was happy with their friendship. Or so she kept telling herself.

Katie tried to concentrate on Stacy. The younger girl was getting ready to do a walkover on the beam, a tricky maneuver that demanded both grace and precision. Even from this distance, Katie could detect a drop of sweat on Stacy's brow as she prepared herself.

"You can do it," Katie murmured. Sure enough, Stacy pulled it off. The crowd in the bleachers burst into spontaneous applause, but Katie knew Stacy didn't even hear it. Katie could tell she was totally caught up in her performance, so much so that she neither saw nor heard anyone around her. For a second, Katie felt like she was the one up there, oblivious to everything but her body and the beam.

Her daydreams were so real that she felt rather than saw someone slide into the seat next to her. But she came back to earth when she heard the familiar, "Hey, K.C."

Greg. Katie smiled up at him. Seeing that sandy hair, those gray-green eyes, the broad smile, she suddenly felt a sad ache in her heart. But she didn't let it show.

"Hi, yourself, Montgomery," she said easily, pushing a strand of long red hair behind an ear. "What's up?"

"Not much," Greg said casually. "Studying for exams, that sort of thing. What about you?"

"Same thing," Katie replied. "I've got a precalculus exam tomorrow. I should probably be home studying for it right now, but I had to see Stacy." She nodded toward the gym floor. "She looks good, don't you think?"

"Yeah," Greg said. "Are you still coaching her?"

Katie nodded.

"That's nice," Greg said.

They were silent for a minute.

"Have you been doing much sailing?" Katie asked, a bit too formally. Sailing was Greg's passion.

"Oh, sure," Greg said. "Whenever I get a chance."

"That's great," Katie said.

Again, they fell silent.

Katie sighed. It was like this every time they met. They talked about lots of things, but never about their relationship. The pain was still there. Maybe they weren't ready for it. Maybe they never would be.

Katie tried to focus on Stacy, but she was so aware of Greg's presence that she couldn't really concentrate. Out of the corner of her eye, she saw him glance at her.

Stacy was preparing to do a handstand on the beam. Katie knew it wasn't an easy move for her, but they'd gone over and over it together. She had to keep her back aligned perfectly to make sure her legs stayed together and formed an absolutely straight line.

24

Katie held her breath as Stacy bent over, her arms perfectly angled. With one flowing movement, she gripped the beam and her legs rose up. Katie examined her form critically. There was just the tiniest bit of wavering in the legs, but hopefully the judges wouldn't count much off for it.

"All set for graduation?" Greg asked, breaking into Katie's thoughts.

She tore her eyes away from Stacy. "Pretty much. It'll feel funny leaving Kennedy."

"Not to mention Rose Hill," Greg added. "When do you have to leave for college?"

Katie hesitated. Finally, she turned to Greg, her expression serious. "I'm not going to the University of Maryland after all."

Greg's eyebrows shot up. "You're kidding! But you got that athletic scholarship!"

Katie nodded. "Yeah, but I don't feel right taking it under the circumstances. I mean, they gave me that scholarship for gymnastics, because they thought I'd be competing for them." She glanced down at her right leg. Katie knew it would never again be as strong as it once was.

For a second, she felt tears sting in her eyes. She blinked rapidly.

"Anyway," she continued, somehow managing to keep her voice steady, "If I took that scholarship now, it would be under false pretenses. So I turned it down and canceled my acceptance."

There was real concern in Greg's voice. "What are you going to do now?"

Katie didn't want Greg to feel sorry for her. She smiled brightly. "Actually, I've been thinking

I might like to become a coach. Maybe I can't compete anymore, but I still love the sport. I think I could be pretty effective. I mean, watching the way Stacy has improved makes me feel like I might have some talent as a coach. It wouldn't be the same as competing myself, but at least I could get a thrill out of seeing my students win."

Greg nodded enthusiastically. "That's a great idea! It would be a shame to waste that competitive spirit."

Katie eyed him warily, and Greg quickly looked away. It was that very same competitive spirit that had brought so much grief to them both. It was still a touchy subject.

"Where are you going to school?" he asked quickly.

Katie sighed. "It's too late to apply to any of the universities that have good coaching programs. I guess I'll have to start off at Rose Hill Community College."

Greg looked disappointed, and Katie knew what he was thinking. RHCC wasn't much of a school. The kids who went there were the ones who couldn't get into better schools, or who just didn't want to leave home.

"Not very exciting, huh?" she continued.

Greg nodded. "It won't be much of a challenge, either. From what I've heard, Rose Hill is like an extension of high school."

"Yeah," Katie said. "But at this point, I don't really have any choice. It's Rose Hill or nothing."

She looked back at Stacy and frowned. Stacy was doing a series of small leaps across the beam, and Katie could tell she was feeling confident —

too confident. This was the point where she usually got a little sloppy. "Point that toe," Katie thought, and then blushed when she realized she'd spoken out loud.

Greg grinned. "You'll be a great coach! And I guess you can always transfer after a year or two at Rose Hill."

"That's true," Katie admitted. "It's just going to feel funny when everyone else takes off this fall and I'm still here."

"Look at the bright side!" Greg said cheerfully. "All of us juniors will still be around, and you've got plenty of friends in our class."

Katie smiled at him. Greg really could be so wonderful sometimes, especially when he knew she was feeling a little low. And he always knew when she was down. He knew her better than anyone else.

These were dangerous thoughts, she warned herself. She couldn't live in the past. Her relationship with Greg was over, and she had to forget it.

She looked down at the gym floor. Stacy was getting ready to dismount. It was a good, clean move, and Katie could see a couple of judges nodding in approval. Now she could relax until it was Stacy's turn on the parallel bars. She turned back to Greg and smiled. "Yeah, it won't be so bad hanging around."

"And we've staked our claim on a great spot at the beach this summer," Greg continued. "We're all going to meet there every weekend."

"That'll be fun," Katie murmured. "It'll be good to see, uh, everyone. . . ." It'll be good to see you, was what she was really thinking. Stop that, she told herself fiercely. But it was no use. Her thoughts were out of control. She looked at Greg. He was looking at her, and she knew he was having the same thoughts. Their eyes locked and suddenly they were gazing into each other's eyes in the old, familiar way. All around them, everything grew hazy and dim. There was no crowd, no Stacy, no gym — just Katie and Greg, alone, together. It was as if nothing had happened, as if nothing between them had changed.

Greg leaned toward her. Almost against her will, Katie felt herself drawing closer to him. With a supreme effort, she pulled back — and the magic of the moment was broken.

Katie looked away, afraid her eyes might betray her and show Greg what she was really feeling. Her heart was pounding so hard she felt certain he could hear it. "I, uh, have to see Stacy before the next event," she mumbled. "Excuse me."

Passing by him on her way to the aisle, she caught a glimpse of his face. He looked surprised, dazed, like something amazing had just happened.

As hard as she tried to push the image out of her mind, his confused look stayed with her as she made her way down to the gym floor.

Chapter
4

When the bell rang after her last class on Friday, Lily breathed a huge sigh of relief. Sitting next to her, Zack McGraw echoed her sigh, and Lily grinned at him.

"The last exam," Lily said thankfully as she gathered up her test papers. "Boy, am I glad *that's* over with!"

"You and me both," Zack agreed. "I feel like celebrating, even though I've still got a composition to write for English."

"I've still got assignments to finish, too," Lily remarked as they walked to the front of the room to drop their exams on the teacher's desk. "I wonder why they have to give final exams two weeks before graduation?"

"I guess so they can get them graded in time," Zack replied. "So they'll know who has to go to summer school to repeat a class."

Lily shuddered. "Summer school! Wouldn't it

29

be awful if you were a senior, thinking you were going to graduate, and you flunked your finals?"

Zack shook his head forcefully. "I wouldn't want to flunk as a junior, either. Summer school is not where I want to spend the next couple of months. Sand and surf is more my style."

Lily laughed. "Yeah, the beach sounds much more appealing to me, too."

"I wish I were there now," Zack said mournfully. "Oh, well, see ya later." He ambled off down the hall, waving as he passed by Jeremy.

The tall, thin, dark-haired boy waved back, and walked rapidly toward Lily. "Hi. I was told we're supposed to go to the Little Theater to pick out the costumes and props for the Senior Follies."

Lily nodded. "Jonathan said to meet him and Diana at his locker."

"The Follies are rather fun, don't you think?" Jeremy asked in his clipped British accent, which Lily found positively enchanting. She made a mental note to study his phrasing, in case she ever got a chance to be in a Shakespeare play. Shakespeare always seemed to sound so much better with an English accent.

"I think so, too," Lily said happily. "I'm so glad I'm getting to work on the show with you guys. I know I can't appear in it, but just working behind the scenes is fun."

Diana was already waiting for them at Jonathan's locker. She greeted them cheerfully. "Where's Jonathan?"

"I don't know," Lily said. "He said to meet him here."

"Maybe he's finishing up an exam," Diana said. "Do you know what class he had last period?"

"I think he had French," Lily replied.

Jeremy groaned. "Then he's probably trying frantically to convince Madame Bouchard to give the class a few more minutes. I had that exam earlier today, and it was really tough. Everyone was still writing when the bell rang. Those verbs! Personally, I don't see how the French manage to learn their own language."

"Poor Jonathan," Lily murmured. For all his outward nonchalance, she knew Jonathan was a serious and conscientious student. Right this minute he was probably going over his exam answers for the zillionth time.

Diana laughed. "Poor Jonathan? Hey, what about the rest of us? We've all been suffering."

"Think about me taking American history," Jeremy added. "I'm the one who deserves your sympathy. You people grew up knowing all that stuff about the Constitution and the Bill of Rights. Not to mention all of those wars!"

Diana's eyes twinkled. "It seems to me that you had a few wars of your own over there in merry old England."

"Yes, I know," Jeremy admitted. "But my point is that *this* country's history is fairly new to me. You guys have an advantage on me."

"He's right," Lily said, smiling at Jeremy. "If I had to learn all of British history in a term, I'd probably go crazy. There's so much to cover! How in the world do you remember all those king and queens?"

Jeremy laughed. "Well, there's one compensation," he told her. "Your history is a lot shorter!" Then he turned to Diana. "What did you think of the political science exam?"

Diana made a face that answered his question before she even spoke. "Gruesome! Especially that essay question!" She laughed heartily. "I could have summed up what I knew in a paragraph, but somehow I managed to stretch it out to two pages. I just hope Mr. Lowell reads it very quickly. If he stops to think about what I wrote, he's going to realize how much of it is trash."

"I did the same thing myself," Jeremy sighed. "I paraphrased each sentence three times." He grinned at Lily. "You'll probably have political science next year. I guarantee you, it's not something to look forward to."

Lily groaned. "I know. I've heard Jonathan complain about it. Seniors are under so much pressure."

"Tell me about it," Diana moaned. "Until we get our finals graded, we don't even know if we're going to graduate!"

"Has a senior ever been held back because they flunked a final exam?" Lily asked, suddenly curious.

Diana grinned. "In one of the Senior Follies skits, the whole football team is held back because they didn't return their equipment. You know, they won't let seniors graduate if they haven't returned school property."

"It doesn't sound like a very funny skit," Lily said doubtfully.

"No, it is," Diana assured her. "You see, the

whole situation turns out to be a plot concocted by the juniors because they don't want the star football players to graduate."

"That's not a bad idea," Jeremy mused. "Although I doubt that Zack McGraw would find it particularly amusing. I think he's looking forward to being next year's star."

Lily glanced at the clock and tapped her foot impatiently. Where *was* Jonathan anyway? Surely he couldn't still be taking that exam. The teachers were pretty strict about making kids turn their tests in when the bell rang.

Jeremy seemed to read her mind. "Maybe Jonathan is involved in one of those infamous senior pranks."

Lily raised her eyebrows. "Senior pranks? Like what?"

"They're an old Kennedy tradition," Diana told her. "Certain seniors have been known to go berserk during the last few weeks of school. I guess it's a way of letting off steam."

"What kinds of pranks to do they pull?" Lily asked.

"Silly things, mostly," Jeremy told her. "Last year someone fiddled around with the computers in the office to make it look as if everyone in the senior class had flunked."

Diana chuckled. "And you know how the secretary reads those announcements every morning over the intercom? Well, last spring someone swiped the official script from her office, and replaced it with a page of gossip — you know, who's dating who, that sort of thing."

Jeremy grinned broadly at the memory. "And the secretary just read them as if they were the real announcements."

Now Lily was laughing, too. It was all pretty dumb stuff, but she could easily see how funny it must have been at the time.

"Hey, here comes Jonathan," Diana said suddenly, waving. Lily turned to see him, and her mouth fell open.

Jonathan definitely didn't look like someone who'd just finished up a wretched French exam. It wasn't just the way he was walking down the hall — slowly, and with a distracted expression — that made him look like he hadn't spent the day at school.

He was wearing brightly flowered baggy shorts, the kind all the boys were wearing at the beach. A towel was tossed over his shoulders, and his hair looked wild and tousled. He was wearing sunglasses, which didn't do much to conceal the fact that his face was bright red. So were his arms and legs.

Lily stared at him in disbelief. "Jonathan! Where have you been?"

Jonathan smiled, but it wasn't his usual grin. There was something uneasy about it, something fake.

"At the beach."

Lily was bewildered. "The beach? What were you doing at the beach?"

Jonathan shrugged lightly. "I just figured it was such a gorgeous day and all that. I didn't feel like being shut up in a classroom."

"It looks like you got a bit of a burn there, old man," Jeremy noted.

Jonathan glanced at his red arms as if he were noticing them for the first time. "Yeah, I guess I did. But it was worth it. The water was great, warm enough for a real swim."

Diana was shaking her head in amusement, but Lily was truly concerned. Although Jonathan's tone was casual, there was something about his whole manner that seemed peculiar. "Jonathan, didn't you have a French final today?"

"Oh, yeah, the French exam." Jonathan took off his sunglasses and rubbed his forehead. "I guess I forgot about it. It's okay, though. I mean, it's really no big deal."

Lily couldn't believe what she was hearing. "No big deal? It was your final exam! Not taking the exam is the same as failing it!"

Jonathan gave her a slight smile, but he wasn't really looking at her. His eyes seemed to be focused over her head.

"I don't think I could fail the course. I've had pretty good grades in French all term." He blinked, then let out a forced laugh. "Besides, Madame Bouchard's a pushover." He struck a cocky pose. "She's crazy about me, you know. I guess I have that effect on certain teachers."

He was just kidding, of course, and Lily knew that. But something about his flippant attitude bothered her. "That's cute, Jonathan," she said dryly. "I had no idea you could snow teachers so easily."

"Especially Madame Bouchard." Jeremy's forehead puckered. "I wouldn't be so confident about charming a good grade out of her if I were you. From what I've seen, I'd say she's rather strict when it comes to grading."

Jonathan didn't look particularly bothered by Jeremy's comment. "Hey, knock it off," he said good-naturedly. "Look, there are only two weeks left of school. No self-respecting senior actually does any work! The sun is shining, the flowers are blooming — "

"And we've got Senior Follies to pull together," Diana reminded him. "Or is *that* too much work for you, too?"

Jonathan grinned. "Nah, that's fun! Let me just stash this towel in my locker and we can take off." As he fiddled with his combination, Lily watched him thoughtfully. What was going on, anyway? Sure, Jonathan liked a good time, but there was something phony about the way he was acting.

Jonathan tossed the towel into his locker. "Okay, let's hit the theater."

"Do you have the keys?" Jeremy asked him.

Jonathan stared at him blankly for a second. "Huh?"

Jeremy raised his eyebrows. "The keys, old chap, the keys . . . to the theater. You were supposed to get them from the custodian today, remember?"

Jonathan smacked his hand against his forehead. "The keys!" he groaned.

"Really, Jonathan," Diana said in a mildly disapproving tone. "I don't know what's gotten into you lately. Missing your exam, forgetting the keys — "

"You know," Jeremy interrupted, "you're going to have to come up with a decent excuse if you want to get Madame Bouchard to give you a make-up exam. Have you thought about that?"

Jonathan wasn't looking at him. He was gazing out the open glass doors toward the quad. "Hey, there's the custodian! Be right back!" Like a bolt of lightning, he went tearing out into the quad.

"A little disorganized lately, wouldn't you say?" Jeremy remarked mildly.

"More than a little," Lily murmured.

"He's probably just got the senior crazies," Diana said, but her voice wasn't very convincing.

"Maybe," Lily agreed doubtfully. She looked out the door at Jonathan chasing after the custodian. Then she turned back to his locker, which Jonathan had left wide open. "I guess I'd better shut this," she said. As she started to close the locker door, she glimpsed inside.

"Good grief!" she exclaimed. "Where did all these books come from?"

Diana glanced inside. "They look like library books. I guess he's working on his English composition."

Jeremy reached in and pulled out a couple of them. He opened one to the back. "If that's true, he's been working on it for a very long time. This book is more than a month overdue." He opened another one. "And this one's two months overdue! Jonathan must really be a slow reader."

Diana pulled out a few more and examined

them. "These are overdue, too." Her expression grew sober as she turned to Lily. "We better remind him about these. He's going to owe a small fortune in overdue fines."

Lily stared at the piles of books jammed into the locker. She was completely bewildered. Jonathan didn't have enough money to throw it away on library fines. And he wasn't the forgetful type, either.

"I don't understand it," she said. "The school library's just around the corner. Why hasn't Jonathan returned these books?"

Jeremy frowned. "He's just being lazy, I suppose. But he'd better get them back fast. Like we were saying before, seniors can't graduate if they haven't returned all school property. That includes library books."

At that moment, Jonathan came bursting back through the glass doors, dangling the keys to the theater in his hand. "Okay, guys, we're all set," he crowed. Then he caught a glimpse of their glum expressions. "Hey, what's going on? Did somebody cancel summer vacation?"

Lily nodded toward the still-open locker. "Jonathan, do you realize you've got a whole bunch of overdue library books in there?"

Jonathan staggered backward three paces and pretended to be shocked. "Overdue library books! Oh, no! Have you called the police yet?" Playfully he grabbed Lily and held her in front of himself. "They'll never take me alive! I've got a hostage!" Then he gently shoved Lily away from him and held her at arms' length. "I've got it!" he went on. "You're the librarian's spy. Your mission is to search all lockers and catch the thieves."

Diana giggled. Jeremy seemed amused, too, but he looked at Jonathan pointedly. "I suppose it's not in the same league as robbing a bank, but you'd better get those books back."

"I will, I will," Jonathan assured them. "Not right this minute, though, okay?"

"You're going to owe the library a ton of money," Diana noted.

Jonathan shrugged. "So I'll owe them a little more."

"When are you going to return them?" Lily persisted.

Jonathan looked at the ceiling and shook his head. "What is this, the Spanish Inquisition? Look, I'll return them, just not right this second. There's still plenty of time before school lets out. I mean, what can they do to me anyway? You think all the librarians are going to gang up on me and beat me with library books?"

Lily looked at him anxiously. "Jeremy says if you don't return them, they won't let you graduate."

Jonathan looked at her seriously. "Don't worry, a few dumb library books aren't going to keep me from graduating." He jangled the theater keys in the air. "Now, can we forget about library books for a little while and get down to something important? On to the Little Theater!"

As if he were leading a parade, Jonathan took off down the hall. Jeremy and Diana looked at each other, shrugged, and followed him.

Lily was right behind them. She tried to put

herself in the proper frame of mind for working on the Follies, but it wasn't easy.

What was wrong with Jonathan? she wondered. One minute he was spacy, as if his mind was someplace far away. The next minute he was horsing around as if he didn't have a care in the world. It wasn't like him to go off to the beach all by himself. And it wasn't like him to miss an exam.

Jonathan knew it, too. Lily could tell that he was uncomfortable about his actions. That's why he was acting so unconcerned, making light of it all.

He's got a problem, Lily thought. And she assured herself he'd either work it out himself or talk to her about it. But even as she tried not to think about it, a little worry settled in the corner of her mind and refused to budge.

Chapter
5

On Wednesday at lunchtime, Karen stood in the cafeteria, looking around for her friends. In one hand, she held her brown-bag lunch, and in the other, she clutched the final edition of *The Red and the Gold*.

As she waited for the other kids, she looked at the newspaper for what must have been the zillionth time. She couldn't help it — she was so proud of what she and the others on the staff had accomplished. The interviews were terrific. They really captured the essence of the class of seniors who would be leading Kennedy High in the fall. And they'd managed to include the name of just about everyone who was involved in an important activity.

Daniel's article on Vincent was particularly good. He'd managed to draw Vince out, something only an excellent reporter could do. Karen didn't know Vince very well, and she suspected very few other kids did, either. He'd struck her as the strong, silent type, the kind of guy who doesn't show what he's feeling and thinking.

But Daniel had asked Vince penetrating questions about his interest in nature. In the interview, Vince had come alive, revealing a side of himself that Karen hadn't known was there. His passion for wildlife and botany was apparent from the enthusiastic responses he'd given Daniel's questions. And while some people might not think nature was the most exciting topic in the world, Daniel had made it truly interesting. Karen herself was amazed to read about the variety of trees in Maryland.

She smiled at a pretty blonde girl in a flowered sundress who was approaching her, also holding a copy of the newspaper.

"Hi, Charlotte," Karen called out. She didn't know Charlotte DeVries very well. She was from Alabama, and she had just started at Kennedy in the spring semester.

"Hey, Karen," Charlotte said. "I just wanted to thank you for saying such nice things about me in the paper. I was so amazed to see my name in print!"

Her soft southern drawl added to the ultra-feminine image she presented. Karen thought Charlotte looked like a dainty, fragile doll. But from what she'd heard from kids who had worked with her on committees, the image was deceiving. Charlotte had shown she was determined and hard-working and had a real talent for solving problems.

"We wanted to do more with you, but there

wasn't enough space to interview everyone," Karen said. "It's too bad, because you deserve it. After all, you're going to be the next student activities director, and that's a major job."

"I hope I can handle it," Charlotte said, smiling brightly.

"Have you talked with Jonathan about what the job involves?" Karen asked.

Charlotte's smile faded slightly. "No, not really. I've tried to talk to him, but he doesn't seem to have time for me right now. I guess he's just real busy with school."

"He's turned over the events calendar to you, hasn't he?"

Charlotte shook her head. "No. I guess it hasn't occurred to him."

Karen frowned. "He should have at least done that by now, even if he doesn't have time to go over it with you. I'll talk to him about it."

"Oh, don't do that," Charlotte said quickly. "I'd hate for him to think I'm bugging him. I'm sure he'll get around to talking to me sooner or later. And listen, I just wanted to tell you, you've done a wonderful job with the newspaper. It's so much more interesting than the one at my old school." She laughed lightly. "And I'd say that even if you hadn't printed my name!" With that, Charlotte waved and walked away.

She was really sweet, Karen decided. But her last words left Karen feeling a little twinge of sadness as she thought about this issue being her last as editor. The newspaper had become such a huge part of her life. Of course, she would definitely work on a newspaper in college, but it wouldn't be the same. On the other hand, if she worked hard, even in the lowliest of positions — proofreading, doing layout, whatever — and she proved her worth, who knows? She might end up as an editor again.

At least she was leaving *The Red and the Gold* in good hands. There were some solid reporters in the junior class, like Daniel . . . *Daniel*. Despite how much she liked his article, Karen frowned. He was obviously the best person on the staff. But a lot of responsibility went with being editor — could Daniel be trusted to handle it? How could she be sure? She had to appoint someone, and she had to do it very soon. The other staff members either didn't want the responsibility, or they weren't organized enough. If not Daniel, then who?

She brushed the disturbing question from her mind and waved as she saw Lily and Jonathan approaching. They were such a cute couple, she thought. For a moment Karen felt wistful — she'd seen so little of her own boyfriend lately. Brian was swamped with some big project, and he was spending a lot of time training Josh to take over the radio station.

"Hi!" Jonathan said as he and Lily joined her. "Let's eat in the quad and pretend we're at the beach."

"Okay," Karen agreed. "It's kind of hot out, though."

Jonathan shrugged as if to say *who cares?* "Like they say, it's not the heat, it's the humidity. And according to my sources, there's a very dry wind blowing."

The three of them ambled down the hall toward the glass doors leading onto the quad. Jonathan was chattering away about nothing in particular. Karen noticed that Lily seemed unusually quiet, and she kept looking at Jonathan apprehensively. What was going on with them? Karen wondered. She hoped they weren't having problems.

Karen's eyes lit up when they started across the quad. Brian was already there.

He looked just as happy to see Karen. "Jonathan said you'd be coming out here for lunch."

"I thought you were spending all your lunch periods working with Josh," Karen told him.

"Yeah, well, I *have* been, but I figured maybe I was hanging over his shoulder too much. Anyway, I told him I was leaving him on his own this period." He pointed to the speaker system. "I can monitor him from here!"

Karen plopped down on one of the benches under the cherry tree. She looked around and sighed. There were so many memories attached to this little plot of land.

"I wonder," she murmured to nobody in particular, "if we come back to this spot in a year, will it still feel special to us? Or will it just be two benches and a cherry tree?"

Brian smiled at her. "It's impossible for me to picture this school without us." He affected a mock-serious look and spoke sternly to Lily. "Next year, at least once a week, I want all you new seniors to observe a moment of silence and think about the seniors who went before you."

Lily saluted him. "Yes, sir!"

45

Karen laughed. "Are you kidding? They'll forget us the minute we're gone. Like they say, out of sight, out of mind."

She glanced at Jonathan as she spoke, and was surprised to see him looking irritated. "Let's not talk about it," he mumbled.

Over the next few minutes, they were joined by Molly, Eric, Katie, Greg, and Holly. Soon it began to seem like a party, with everyone trading sandwiches, passing around sodas, and all talking at once. It was as if all the senior members of the crowd were aware that their days there were numbered, that they wouldn't have many more times like this when they'd all be together, and they were trying to make the most of it.

Especially Jonathan. Karen had never seen him quite so happy, laughing and joking with everyone, the absolute life of the party.

"Why is *he* coming over here?" Brian muttered to Karen. Karen looked to see who he was talking about, and sighed a little when she realized it was Daniel striding over toward them. Brian had never quite forgiven Daniel for the prank he'd pulled on Karen. When Karen had first realized what Daniel had done to her, she'd been panic-stricken. Brian, in his usual laid-back way, had tried to calm her down. But she was so upset, they'd ended up having a huge fight. Eventually they got back together, but as Brian's narrowed eyes observed Daniel's approach, Karen knew he'd never forget the problems Daniel had caused. Karen wondered if *she* could. . . .

Daniel sat down on the bench next to Karen and beamed at her. "I've been getting compliments all day on my interview with Vince," he told her. Karen smiled and nodded. One thing about Daniel — he definitely wasn't shy about blowing his own horn.

"It's a good piece," she remarked.

"Do you really think so?" Daniel asked eagerly, looking as if Karen's opinion was the only thing in the world that truly mattered.

"Sure," Karen said honestly. "You're an excellent reporter. Oh, and I wanted to thank you for editing Emily's article and the round-up section. I could never have done all of them and studied for finals, too."

"What did you think of my editing?" Daniel asked.

Karen paused. She knew what Daniel was really asking, and she wasn't sure how to reply. "Nice job," she said carefully. "I know Emily's grammar isn't always the greatest in the world, so it couldn't have been easy."

"So you think I've got solid editorial skills?" Daniel persisted.

Brian, who had been listening to this conversation, burst out in an annoyed tone, "Hey, she said it was a nice job, okay? Isn't that enough? What do you want, a trophy or something?"

Daniel's eyes darted back and forth between Karen and Brian, and Karen managed a weak smile. Frantically she looked around for an excuse to change the subject.

"There's Vince," she said brightly, waving and beckoning to the muscular, dark-haired boy who had just wandered into the quad.

Vince looked a little surprised by Karen's enthusiastic greeting, but he smiled slightly and started over to them.

"Join us," Karen said to him.

"Thanks," Vince said, looking around for a place to sit.

"There's room here," Molly said. "Let me just clear away some of this junk," She started gathering up the empty bags, but Vince stopped her.

"Don't worry, I'll do it," he said pleasantly. Katie started to get up off the ground to make room for him, and Vince took her elbow to help her.

He was a real gentleman, Karen thought. He seemed like the type who needed a damsel in distress to rescue. No wonder he enjoyed being a volunteer fireman.

"Hey, listen up, kids," Brian said. Josh's voice came over the quad, loud and clear.

"Here's a little something especially for you seniors out there. Good luck out there in the real world, folks. We're going to miss you. This golden oldie is dedicated to you."

Karen remembered the song well. It was the number one hit the summer before she entered Kennedy High. The sweet, soft ballad about going far away and leaving someone you love had just been a great slow dance tune at the time. Now it carried a special meaning.

Most of the kids grew quiet, smiles on their faces. Karen knew they were all feeling the mixture of emotions she was experiencing — pleasure from the happy memories the song brought back, a little sadness brought on by the wistful lyrics. But even as she drifted blissfully with the tune,

Karen couldn't help noticing that Jonathan was the only one who didn't seem to share the spirit. He was looking around restlessly.

Karen leaned back on the bench, Brian put his arm around her, and she closed her eyes. The song ended, and a peaceful, relaxed feeling seemed to come over the group. The mood didn't last, though.

"Oh, no," Karen heard someone mutter grimly. Reluctantly she opened her eyes.

Heading toward them was Roxanne. Even from this distance, Karen could see her wide-set green eyes flashing. Her lips were set in a thin line, and her beautiful face was taut with rage.

She was carrying a copy of *The Red and the Gold* and, as she drew closer, Karen could see that the knuckles on the hand she clutched it with had turned white.

Everyone was watching her with expressions that ranged from a mild uneasiness to downright distaste. When Karen realized Rox's angry eyes were focused on *her*, she felt positively sick. What was that girl so steamed up about?

She found out soon enough. Before Karen could even say hello, Roxanne lit into her. She practically shoved the newspaper in Karen's face. "Do you call this fair reporting?" she demanded.

Karen blinked. "I, uh . . . I don't know what you mean."

Rox's gaze swept over the group spread out on the benches and lawn. "I thought you guys were supposed to be so friendly and open to new people. At least that's what the other Stevenson kids have been telling me. When I first transferred here, I had a feeling you guys were a closed crowd, and I warned the Stevenson kids about that. But they kept saying, 'Roxanne, give them a chance. They're not so bad.' So I did! I volunteered to work on all your stupid committees! But you guys act like I'm not even alive!"

Karen didn't know what to say. She wasn't even sure she knew what Roxanne was talking about.

Daniel was looking at Roxanne, his forehead slightly wrinkled. "Roxanne, calm down. Why are you picking on Karen, anyway? What does she have to do with all this?"

"She's the newspaper editor, isn't she?" Roxanne snapped. "Editors are supposed to be fair, right?" She opened the paper. "Well, if that's true, how come there are photos here of, let's see: Greg, Lily, Stacy, Josh, even Vincent, and there's *nothing* about me and my position."

She crumpled up the newspaper and threw it to the ground. "Maybe you don't realize that I'm supposed to be clubs editor for the yearbook next year. Or maybe you just don't care. Maybe that job isn't considered outstanding enough for you people." She practically spat out those last words, and Karen almost jumped out of her seat. She looked wildly at Brian, but he seemed just as surprised.

Daniel wasn't, though. He spoke to Roxanne seriously and calmly. "We couldn't put in pictures of everyone, Rox. There just wasn't enough space."

Roxanne's eyes were blazing. "Forget the pictures! There wasn't any mention of me at all! It

50

seems to me that being clubs editor of the yearbook is a pretty important position. At least as important as — as — as the Wilderness Club!"

Her tone made it clear she thought the Wilderness Club was about the dumbest activity in school, and Karen glanced apprehensively at Vince to see his reaction. Vince didn't seem particularly disturbed by Roxanne's remark. If anything, he was looking at Roxanne with concern, almost as if he felt sorry for her.

"Gee, Roxanne, I'm really sorry about that," Daniel said in a soothing voice. "It must have been a mistake."

Karen finally found her voice. "That's right. I mean, we didn't leave you out on purpose. There were just so many activities and people to cover. . . ." Under Roxanne's glare, she squirmed a little and her voice trailed off.

Daniel, however, didn't seem the least bit intimidated. "It really wasn't intentional, Rox. You shouldn't take it so personally."

Karen had to admire his take-charge approach, and the sensible way he was handling this. For a second, it actually looked as though Roxanne might calm down. Then Jonathan opened his big mouth.

"What difference does it make, Roxanne? You're acting like all you want is a little bit of recognition. Hah! You wouldn't have been happy seeing your name in print. You wouldn't have been satisfied if the whole newspaper was about you!"

Roxanne gasped and Karen groaned. She'd forgotten that Jonathan was still holding a grudge about the way Rox had used him at the Valentine's Day Dance. Now what would Roxanne do? she wondered. Scream at them for the rest of lunch period?

But Jonathan's blunt remark seemed to have taken the fight out of her. All Roxanne did was give them all one last angry, disgusted look. Then she whirled around and stormed out of the quad.

Vince stared at Rox as she hurried away. Even in her anger, Roxanne was beautiful, breathtaking. And she had every right to be angry, he thought, if what she said was true. Had the Kennedy kids snubbed her since the day she arrived? Vince doubted it. As far as he could tell, they all seemed really friendly. He only knew them through Josh, but they appeared to be a pretty down-to-earth bunch.

On the other hand, he supposed the student leaders might seem exclusive to an outsider. Even though they weren't snobs at all, someone who didn't know them might think they were. But even if the crowd hadn't snubbed her, Roxanne obviously felt like they had. She struck Vince as lonely and sad, someone who desperately wanted friends. The anger was just a cover-up.

How could Jonathan have insulted her like that? No gentleman should talk to a lady that way. He must have hurt her terribly to make her run off like that.

Suddenly he jumped to his feet. "Excuse me," he murmured to the others as he hurried out of the quad.

* * *

Walking rapidly down the dirt path that led to the athletic field, Roxanne shook with fury. How dare they treat her like that? How dare they!

She heard someone running up behind her, but she didn't bother to turn around to see who it was. Then she noticed Vincent was walking alongside her.

"What do *you* want?" she asked harshly.

Vince stood there stiffly, looking terribly serious. "I want to apologize."

Rox stared at him in surprise. "Apologize? You? What are you apologizing for?"

"For taking up so much room in the newspaper," Vince explained. "I guess I talked too much. If I hadn't, there probably would have been room for your interview."

Roxanne glared at him. "Nobody bothered to interview me at all."

"But I'm sure they would have put in something about you if they had had the space."

"Don't count on it," Roxanne said.

"I'm sure they didn't leave you out on purpose," Vince continued. "And my interview was much too long. You see, after we finished talking about my plans for the Wilderness Club, Daniel asked me about my work with the volunteer firefighters. I guess I get carried away when I start talking about it. It gets pretty exciting."

"I'll bet," Roxanne muttered sarcastically.

Vince didn't seem to pick up on her tone. "Honestly, Roxanne," he said sincerely. "It wasn't right that your name was left out. And I'm sure that right this minute those guys feel really awful about it."

Roxanne's mouth dropped open. Was this guy for real? If he believed what he was saying, he must be even more dense than she'd suspected.

She searched Vince's face for any indication that he was putting her on, that this was some kind of an act. But his face was open and honest.

Then it dawned on her. Vince probably didn't have the slightest idea of what had been going on the whole term! After all, he didn't really hang out with the others — at least, Rox had never seen him with any of them but Josh. And Josh hadn't really been friendly with them for that long.

Maybe Vincent didn't know about her history, about how she'd toyed with Jonathan and Eric and Greg. Maybe he didn't know anything about the Kennedy–Stevenson feud she'd created.

It was all becoming clear now. Vince was a wide-eyed innocent, a babe in the woods.

Too bad he was also a dork. And Roxanne was in no mood to deal with dorks — not even sincere ones.

"Look, just leave me alone, okay?" She turned away from him. Just as she did, a hot, dry gust of wind blew a bit of dirt in her eye. As her eye started to sting, she covered it with her hand.

"Are you all right?" Vince asked.

Tentatively Roxanne took her hand from her eye. It was still burning and watering, and she felt a tear slowly trickle down her cheek.

She was aware that Vince was watching her. "Are you okay?" he asked again.

She was about to tell him that she had something in her eye when she caught sight of his expression. That stiff, polite look was gone. There was serious concern on his face, real sympathy. She realized with a jolt that Vince thought she was crying!

What a jerk, she thought, and almost started laughing. But she caught herself just in time. And her devious mind immediately went to work.

So Vince thought she was crying over the way the crowd had treated her. Well maybe she could use his concern to her advantage. She turned away from him, as if she were ashamed for him to see her tears, and put a hand to her eyes. As Vince placed a tentative, comforting hand on her shoulder, Rox began planning feverishly.

Vincent could definitely be her ticket into the crowd. He'd just started hanging out with them, and he obviously knew nothing about her past. Jonathan and Eric and a lot of the other guys were graduating, and they'd be out of her way. True, a couple of the juniors — Greg, for one — weren't too crazy about her, but she'd always suspected it was mostly Jonathan and his friends who were still stinging from her flirtations and determined to keep her out of the crowd. And Katie, of course. She was still resentful about that little fling Rox had had with Greg, not to mention the skiing accident. But Katie was graduating, too.

Rox could start her senior year with an almost-clean slate. And if she could grab onto Vince, she could get in good with next year's crowd, even if it meant coming in on his coattails. Trying to look like a shy little lamb, she gave him a sidelong glance, taking the opportunity to examine him critically.

Okay, he wasn't her idea of a heartthrob. He was definitely not her type at all, and the thought of being locked in a passionate embrace with him left her cold. But she could fake it for a while — for long enough to get firmly established in the crowd, anyway. Once that happened, she'd find someone better and dump Vince. She could tell he was the gullible, naive type. It shouldn't be too difficult to use him. She'd already tossed the bait. Now all she had to do was pull him in.

She rested her cheek on his muscular shoulder.

"It's been so hard for me here," she said softly, "being a new kid and all. I really have no one I can talk to. It's — it's been so lonely."

"Gosh, that's too bad," Vincent said. "Have you really tried to get to know people? Most of those kids are pretty nice, I think."

"I've tried, really I have," Rox murmured. She gave a couple of little sniffs so he'd think she was still crying. If only she could force a few more tears. "Those kids just don't like me."

"I don't understand," Vince said. "Why wouldn't they like you?"

"I don't know," Rox said forlornly. "It just seems like everything I say or do gets misunderstood. You heard what Jonathan said just now."

Vince's voice hardened. "That was pretty mean. He shouldn't have spoken to you like that."

Roxanne sighed. "It's just that I was so hurt at being left out. And Jonathan makes it sound like all I want is lots of attention; like I'm some sort of show-off. I'm really not, but I was just so upset, I didn't even know what I was saying."

Vince nodded. "Like you said, maybe Jonathan misunderstood you. I'm sure he didn't really want to hurt your feelings like that."

Sure, he didn't, Roxanne thought grimly. Jonathan meant exactly what he said. But she didn't let her thoughts show on her face. Instead, she cocked her head to one side, looked meaningfully at Vince and batted her eyelashes.

"I'm not such a bad person," she said sweetly. "I hope you don't think I'm a show-off."

Vince shook his head. "Not at all."

"You know, I really want to make friends here at Kennedy," Rox continued. "I guess I just don't know how to do it."

"I know what you mean," Vince said. "I'm kind of a loner myself. For a long time, Josh was my only real friend here. It's only because of him that I've started to get to know the other kids."

"I'm sure they all think you're terrific," Rox gushed. She wished she could force a blush. This would be the perfect moment. "There's something about you. . . ."

Vincent looked at her blankly. "What do you mean?"

Rox chose her words carefully. After all, she didn't want to come on *too* strong. "Well, you seem so much more mature than other juniors. And strong. You seem like the kind of guy a girl could depend on."

That should appeal to his macho instincts, she

thought. Sure enough, Vince's eyes shone with pleasure. Not only that, she discovered *he* could blush.

I can have him if I want him, she thought. I've just got to play my cards right. She tossed her head so her red hair swung across her shoulders, and smiled warmly at him. "Thank you for listening to my craziness," she said. "I only wish the other kids were as understanding as you are."

"Maybe they are," Vince said thoughtfully. "To tell you the truth, I really don't know them that well. But Josh likes them a lot, and I can't imagine that Josh would like people who were snobbish or unkind."

"How do they act toward you?"

Vince grinned. "They've been really friendly. That's probably just because I'm Josh's friend —"

"Oh, no," Roxanne objected. "I'm sure they like you for yourself."

Vince shrugged. "I don't know. All I know is that they've pretty much welcomed me with open arms, acting like I've always been one of them."

"That's nice," Roxanne said.

Vince cocked his head and looked at her thoughtfully. "I'll bet you just need to get to know them better."

"Maybe you're right," Roxanne said. "But how?"

"They invited me to join them at the beach this weekend. Maybe you should come, too."

Roxanne faked a look of horror. "By myself? Oh, I couldn't, I just couldn't. Not after what happened today."

Then, as if the memory had just refueled her

grief, she put her hand to her eyes and pretended to weep again.

"Don't cry," Vince said, putting his arm lightly about her shoulders. "It won't be that bad. I'll be there. Why don't you come?"

Was he asking her for a date? Roxanne waited to see if he'd say anything like, "I'll pick you up and bring you." When he didn't, she decided not to say anything. After all, she didn't want to sound pushy. Guys like Vince didn't like pushy girls — they liked to do all the chasing themselves. Roxanne had to let him think he was chasing her.

"I'll think about it," she said. "I honestly don't think I could face them on my own. But maybe if you're there, it won't be so scary."

Vince nodded solemnly. "It's almost time for class," he said. "Here, let me carry your books."

Roxanne obediently handed them over. Together, they headed back to school.

Chapter
6

Lily stood in front of Jonathan's locker, tapping her foot impatiently and glancing at her watch. He was only a few minutes late, but she was beginning to wonder if maybe he'd forgotten they were supposed to meet there. He'd been so out of it lately, so not himself . . . she just hoped he hadn't taken off again and gone to the beach.

Looking at the locker made her wonder if those overdue library books were still inside. She could always ask him if he'd returned them, remind him at least. But the more she thought about it, the more she knew she couldn't ask. Jonathan's moods were getting so unpredictable; one minute he'd be clowning and acting crazy, the next minute he'd be so touchy he'd jump down her throat if she looked at him funny.

And she still had no idea what was going on. Something had to be bothering him. Problems at home, maybe, or trouble in a class. . . . Who knew? Until he was ready to talk about it, there was nothing she could do.

Lily sighed in relief when she saw him coming down the hall. He was dressed normally, in khakis and a shirt, which meant he'd probably been in school all day. He was smiling, too. That was a good sign.

"Hi!" he called to her. "Look, I'm starving. Let's go get a pizza."

Lily rolled her eyes. "Jonathan! It's Thursday!"

"Huh?" He looked at her blankly.

"We've got a rehearsal for the Senior Follies, remember? Everyone's probably at the Little Theater waiting for us right this minute."

Jonathan groaned. "Oh, yeah, I forgot." Then he brightened. "Well, this ought to be fun. I just hope you know what you're doing, because I sure don't." He smiled at her in that wonderful, boyish way that made her heart melt. When he looked at her like that, she could forgive him for anything.

He draped an arm casually around her shoulders, and together they headed toward the Little Theater. As Lily suspected, most of the other kids were already there.

"Sorry we're late," Jonathan called out. Lily looked around and tried not to feel apprehensive. She was the only junior there among the dozen kids who were involved in the Follies.

No one seemed to mind, though.

"I'm glad you're here helping us," Diana Einerson told her. "We know our lines and all that, but we don't have the slightest idea what to do once we're onstage."

"And I've got a pretty good feeling old Jonathan doesn't know, either," Brian piped up.

"Which is exactly why I brought in a theatrical expert to help us," Jonathan said. He beamed down at Lily. His tone was cheerful and easy-going, but Lily couldn't help feeling that it sounded forced, as if he were trying very hard to sound cheerful. Resolutely, Lily pushed her concerns aside for the moment. Right now she had to cope with this new responsibility.

"Well, I'm not exactly Woody Allen," she confessed. "But I'll do what I can. Of course," she added hastily, "I'm just the assistant director. Jonathan is still the final authority."

"Did you read the skits?" Molly asked her.

Lily nodded. "I think they're hysterical! I was laughing out loud just reading them."

Jonathan slumped down on a chair, pulling down his fedora so it half-covered his eyes. "Okay. Let's get started."

"Which skit do you think should go first, Lily?" Jeremy asked.

"I think you need to start off with something really strong, one of the skits that has a big cast. It'll put the audience in the right frame of mind." She turned to Jonathan. "Don't you think so?"

"Yeah, sure, whatever you say," Jonathan replied with a wave of his hand. Once again, his thoughts seemed to be far away.

"What about 'If the Seniors Ran the School'?" Karen suggested. "That's got a lot of people in it."

"That's my choice, too," Lily said. She picked up a script and scanned it. "Okay, we'll need six chairs on the stage, in two rows."

As Brian and Jeremy began arranging the chairs, Lily checked the script again. "Karen, Brian, Molly, Matt, Diana, and Holly," she read out loud. "You guys sit in the chairs. Jeremy, you're the teacher."

Everyone obediently went to their places. Then they all turned and looked expectantly at Lily.

"Look straight at the teacher, as if you were in class," Lily instructed. They did. Jeremy, standing in front of them, looked uncomfortable.

"This feels kind of peculiar," he mumbled. Lily examined him critically.

"I know, you need something to make you feel like a teacher," she said. She went over to a table where bits and pieces of costumes and props were scattered. She selected some wire-rimmed glasses and a fake moustache.

"Put these on," she ordered Jeremy. With a look of extreme reluctance, he did as he was told.

The effect made the rest of the kids burst out laughing.

"Calm down," Lily told them sternly. "The audience is supposed to do the laughing, not you. Now Jeremy, you're a math teacher. I want you to look very serious. Everyone know their lines?"

There was a general bobbing of heads.

"All right, then," Lily said. "Molly, you start."

Molly turned. "Welcome to Kennedy High's annual Senior Follies, our last chance to make serious fools of ourselves before we face the real world. Now, I'm sure you're all aware that seniors complain about their course loads more than anyone else. If we were in charge, classes would be conducted a lot differently. In this skit, we're

63

going to show you how a typical class day would be if the seniors ran the school."

She faced forward again. Jeremy stood up stiffly and spoke in a monotone. "In math today, we have an important lesson to learn. We are going to discuss numbers."

"Numbers!" Matt called out. "Whew! What a concept!"

Jeremy stared at him for a second. Then he turned, embarrassed, to Lily. "Sorry. I seem to have forgotten my next line."

Lily checked the script. " 'Since there are so many numbers available — ' "

"Ah, yes," Jeremy said. Then he frowned. "I feel silly just standing here. I wish there were something I could do with my hands."

Lily had an idea. "You know that algebra teacher who keeps taking off his glasses and cleaning them during class? Why don't you do that?"

"That's good!" Karen said.

Everyone was looking at Lily approvingly.

"What do you think, Jonathan? Do you think that's a good idea?" Lily asked. When he didn't reply, she turned to look at him. His eyes were half-closed. He wasn't asleep — he just looked as if he'd been caught in the middle of some heavy-duty thinking.

"Jonathan?" Lily asked again.

He blinked and looked up at her. "Huh?"

"Do you think that's a good idea?"

From his expression, Lily could tell he didn't have the slightest idea what she was talking about, but he nodded anyway.

"Yeah, sure, it's a great idea."

Lily stared at him for a moment, then turned back to the kids onstage. "Okay, let's take it from 'What a concept!' "

Matt repeated his line. Jeremy took off his glasses and cleaned them. He looked much more relaxed.

"Since there are so many numbers available," he said, "we're only going to deal with the first five. Actually, I don't think we have to talk about one at all, since it's boring. We shall begin with two." He paused, cleared his throat, and held up two fingers.

"Two is company," he intoned dramatically. The others pretended to be copying that down, as if they were taking notes.

"Any questions?" Jeremy asked. When there were none, he continued. "Three's a crowd. Four is a double date. And five is a party."

"How are we supposed to remember all this?" Molly asked, groaning.

"Yes, I realize it's a great deal of work," Jeremy replied. "So that will be all for today."

"Good!" Lily said. "Now it's current events, and Molly's the teacher." As Jeremy and Molly began to trade places, Lily frowned. "I wonder if there's some way we could show that you're changing classes. Jonathan, do you have any ideas?"

"Huh? Oh, no, I don't have any ideas," he mumbled.

Lily looked at him curiously. He didn't even seem to be paying attention. She turned back to the stage and thought for a moment.

"How about this? At the end of each class, someone will ring a bell off stage. Everyone gets up, walks around the chairs in a circle, then goes back to their seats like in Musical Chairs. It'll look kinda silly, but that's the point."

There was a general chorus of okays, and they tried it.

"Looks good," Lily said, mentally patting herself on the head for coming up with the idea. "Okay, Molly, go."

"In current events today, we have important issues to discuss. To begin, it has been reported that a number of Kennedy senior females are involved in relationships with several Kennedy junior males. Does this represent a significant cultural phenomenon? Does it indicate an unusual level of maturity on the part of Kennedy boys — or should I say, men? Conversely, does this fact suggest that Kennedy women wish to dominate their dates? Or perhaps their interest in junior males is due simply to the fact that the senior males aren't worth pursuing. We can only speculate as to the reasons. Where this trend will lead is open to debate. That is all for today."

"Ring, ring," Lily shouted. On cue, everyone got up, walked around the chairs, and sat down again. This time Karen was in front.

"Knowledge of history is very important," she said. "In order to understand the events of today, we must know what happened in the past. For example, did you know that Katie used to go out with Eric? They were a steady couple until Katie met Greg."

Holly raised her hand and waved it frantically. "But Greg and Eric are friends! How can that be?"

"That is one of the great mysteries of the universe," Karen replied solemnly.

"Wow," Diana remarked. "Knowing history really *is* important. I understand so much more now than I did before."

"Very good," Karen said. "Class dismissed."

The next episode was an English class, which was spent analyzing a *Rolling Stone* magazine. This was followed by sociology, in which the class discussed the cultural significance of miniskirts.

Before the last "class" began, Brian declared, "Boy, I'm glad we've got PE now. I'm sick of all this heavy academic stuff."

"Yes, indeed," Jeremy agreed. "I feel like getting into something really physical."

As the teacher, Matt, went up front, he said, "Today we are practicing an exercise in which you should be involved at least eight hours a day. To begin, stretch your arms out to the side. Then take a deep breath through your mouth."

He demonstrated the exercise, performing an exaggerated yawn. The students followed his example.

"Next, place your arms on your desk and lower your head until it rests on your arms. Now, slowly let your eyelids drop until your eyes are completely closed. You are now in the proper position. Ready? Begin sleeping."

Lily clapped her hands. "Terrific!"

Behind her, Jonathan was applauding, too.

Lily wondered just how much of the skit he'd actually heard. Well, at least he was smiling. "Why don't you do the Valentine's Day Dance routine next?" he suggested.

"Okay," Lily agreed, pleased that he was showing some interest. "That's just Molly and Brian, with Karen doing the introduction. We need to push the chairs out of the way."

They were in the process of setting up when Brian stopped and squinted toward the back of the auditorium. "Isn't that Mr. Barnes?" he asked.

Lily turned and barely made out the figure of the English teacher. "Looks like him," she said. Glancing at Jonathan, she was surprised to see him go suddenly pale.

"Excuse me," he murmured. "I, uh, need to get something backstage." He headed quickly onstage and behind the curtain before Mr. Barnes could see him.

"Hey, Mr. Barnes," Brian called out to the teacher. "Are you here to get a sneak preview? If so, I'd better warn you, it's not exactly a theatrical masterpiece."

Mr. Barnes smiled slightly, but his eyes were serious. "I'm looking for Jonathan Preston. I heard he was here."

"I'll get him," Lily said quickly. She went backstage to find Jonathan just standing there, staring into space.

"Jonathan," she began tentatively. He almost jumped at the sound of her voice.

"What?"

"Mr. Barnes wants to see you." She looked at him quizzically, wondering why he seemed so reluctant to see one of his favorite teachers. But he just nodded and went back out to the front. Lily followed him.

"Over here, Mr. Barnes. What's up?" His tone was light and easygoing, but Lily detected a hint of nervousness.

"I'd like to speak with you privately for a moment," Mr. Barnes said.

"Sure thing!" Jonathan led him over to an area behind a stack of props.

Lily watched them, her forehead lined with worry. Jonathan certainly didn't look particularly concerned. But Mr. Barnes looked dead serious.

"Uh, let's take a break," she called out to the kids on the stage. "I want to check some props."

She wandered over to the stack of props, positioning herself where neither Jonathan nor Mr. Barnes could see her, hoping to "accidentally overhear" what they were saying. *Something* was going on — and she had to know what it was if she was going to help Jonathan.

"I want to talk to you about the final paper for my course," Mr. Barnes was saying.

"Final paper?" Jonathan's voice was flat.

"Do I really need to remind you?" Mr. Barnes sounded impatient. "You were asked to write a ten-page composition about what it means to graduate and go out into the real world. It was due two days ago, and you haven't turned it in."

"Oh, *that* paper!" Jonathan paused. "To tell you the truth, Mr. Barnes, I've given it a lot of thought, and I think it's a waste of time to try and guess what life will be like after high school."

He sounded as if he were making a joke, but

Mr. Barnes wasn't laughing. If anything, the English teacher seemed annoyed.

"It may seem like a waste of time to you, Jonathan, but it is an assignment. And I expect it to be completed. Everyone else in your class has written this essay. I don't know what makes you think you can be an exception."

"Because I'm an exceptional kind of guy!" Jonathan's voice was strangely flippant. It was a crack he might make among his friends, but it certainly wasn't the way he usually talked to teachers. "Look, Mr. Barnes, try to see it my way. I mean, how can I write about what it means to graduate when I haven't done it yet?"

There was a moment of silence before Mr. Barnes spoke again. "Jonathan, I must admit I'm a bit taken aback by your attitude. You've been one of my best students, and I don't understand why you're behaving this way. Is there something you'd like to talk about?"

Jonathan's laugh sounded artificial. "No, everything's great, absolutely terrific. Look, I've got an idea. How about if I wait until after graduation and *then* write your composition? Okay?"

Lily couldn't believe what she was hearing. How could Jonathan act like that in front of a teacher?

Mr. Barnes obviously wasn't amused. When he spoke, his voice was steady and firm. "You may consider it a joke, Jonathan, but this is the most important assignment of the term. It counts for half your grade. Now, because you've always been a good student, I'm giving you a break. You have until Tuesday to turn in that essay. If it is not turned in to me by then, you will receive a failing grade. Which means, of course, that you will *not* be graduating."

With that, Mr. Barnes turned and walked briskly to the door. Quickly, Lily went back to the stage area, the teacher's words still ringing in her ears. Not graduate? How could Jonathan have gotten himself into such a mess? He was always so conscientious about his assignments. Why hadn't he written that essay?

She was frantic with concern. And when Jonathan rejoined the group, she could tell he was upset, too. Even with his tan, he looked pale.

But even if he was visibly distressed, he didn't let it show in his manner. "Okay, let's get this show on the road! Who's in the Valentine's Day Dance skit?"

"Brian and I are the stars of this one," Molly said lightly.

"Right, good," Jonathan said. "Um, so go ahead and get started."

"Lily, where do you think we should stand at the beginning?" Molly asked.

Lily was staring at Jonathan. He should be home writing that essay!

Molly repeated her question, and Lily tore her eyes away from Jonathan.

"You should stand on one side of the stage and Brian should be on the other," she said quickly, then turned back to Jonathan. "Jonathan," she said in a low voice, "if you've got, uh, other things to do, I can handle this by myself. I mean, you don't really need to be here."

71

"No way!" Jonathan said spiritedly. "You've been doing all the work so far. It's about time I started carrying my share of the load."

"I don't mind — " Lily began. But Jonathan wasn't paying any attention to her. He had a smile fixed on his face as he focused on the stage. "Karen, you go ahead and make the introduction."

Karen went to the center of the stage. "Last February, Kennedy High held a Valentine's Day Dance, where dates were set up by computer. Boys and girls were matched up according to common interests. But we were wondering — what if there had been a glitch in the program? What kind of couples would have been matched up? Here's a little dramatization of what might have happened at the Valentine's Day Dance."

Molly came out from the side of the stage. "I wonder who my date is," she said. "I've got my secret code word. It's — " She stopped. Then she turned apologetically to Lily. "I forgot the code word."

At Molly's words, Lily had an inspiration. "Listen, you're all probably tired. Why don't we call it off for today? I know you've got other stuff to do. I mean, we've all still got homework and projects and assignments to finish. You know, like *essays*." As she spoke she looked pointedly at Jonathan, but he didn't seem to notice.

"I'm not tired," he said quickly. "I can keep going. How about you guys? Are any of you ready to quit?"

"Not particularly," Matt remarked. "Hey, by the way, what did Barnes want?"

Jonathan shrugged. "Nothing much." He picked up a script and began fumbling through it. "Molly, the code word is 'sauerkraut.' "

Matt was looking at Jonathan curiously. "He looked like it was something important."

"What are you talking about?" Jonathan asked.

"Barnes! He seemed like he had something really urgent to talk to you about."

Jonathan shrugged. "No big deal."

Lily couldn't keep silent any longer. "No big deal? He said you hadn't turned in your composition!"

Jonathan didn't look particularly angry about her knowing his secret. He just shrugged again. "Don't worry about it. It's nothing to get all worked up about."

"Still, you'd better get it in," Brian said mildly. "Barnes is pretty strict."

"He was just giving me grief," Jonathan said. "He's not all that steamed. You know how he likes to act important and throw his weight around. He's just enjoying his last few days of pushing us seniors around."

"Don't count on it," Karen warned him. "Barnes means what he says."

"What kind of essay is it?" Jeremy asked. "Not your final composition, I hope."

"Nah," Jonathan muttered. "Come on, let's get back to the skit."

"Wait a minute," Brian said. "Is that the essay he assigned at the beginning of the term, the one on graduating and going out into the world?"

"That's the one," Jonathan said. "Pretty stupid topic, right?"

"Maybe it's stupid," Brian remarked, "but it counts for fifty percent of your grade! It's the *final*."

By now everyone had gathered around Jonathan, and their faces all reflected concern. "Fifty percent!" Diana exclaimed. "Jonathan, if you don't turn in that essay, you could fail the course!"

"And if you fail the course," Jeremy noted, "you won't graduate!"

Jonathan's eyes were troubled, but he covered it up with a laugh. "Hey, you guys, knock it off! Barnes is just bluffing. He's not going to stop me from graduating. How would it look if the student activities director didn't graduate?"

Lily shook her head in bewilderment. "Jonathan, what's the matter with you? You have to take this seriously! Graduation is a week from Saturday!"

Jonathan finally stopped smiling. His whole expression changed. Suddenly his eyes narrowed, and he glared at Lily coldly. "Since when do I have to take advice from a dumb junior?"

Lily was in shock. Jonathan had never spoken to her like that before.

"She's right — " Molly began.

This time Jonathan exploded.

"Look, I'm getting sick of all this nagging, okay? I know what I'm doing, and I don't need to listen to this! Why can't you all just leave me alone! Just shut up and leave me alone!" He threw his script on the floor and all the pages scattered.

Stunned and shaken, Lily watched in despair as he stormed out of the Little Theater.

Chapter
7

Late Saturday morning, still in her bathrobe, Roxanne wandered into the kitchen. She opened the refrigerator and examined the contents. It didn't take long because there wasn't much to examine. Grocery shopping was not one of her mother's favorite activities, and the nearly empty fridge was evidence of that.

There were a couple of wilted stalks of celery, an old, unappealing apple, and a container of onion dip that was probably spoiled. In the door were half a lime, a lemon, and two jars — one containing a few maraschino cherries, the other holding green olives. Rox pulled out the jar of olives, unscrewed the lid, and popped one in her mouth. Great breakfast.

She retied her bathrobe tighter around her waist and checked through some cabinets. Nothing much there. Her eye was caught by a box lying on the counter, and she peered inside. A couple of slices of cold pizza lay forlornly on the greasy paper. Torrey must have ordered it last night.

As if on cue, her brother ambled into the kitchen. "Hey, don't touch my breakfast," he muttered. He grabbed a slice out of the box. "What's the matter, no hot date today?"

"Oh, shut up and get out of here," Rox growled. She was in no mood for his usual insults.

But Torrey was enjoying himself. "Let's see, what is this now, the third dateless weekend in a row?"

"Get out of here!" Rox screamed. Torrey laughed, grabbed the other slice of pizza, and took off.

He certainly hadn't done anything to improve her mood. Aimlessly Rox's gaze wandered around the kitchen and came to rest on a wall calendar. She noticed her mother's handwriting on that day's square and read it: *Brunch with Ambassador Westner, 11:00* A.M.

Typical, she thought. At this very moment her mother was probably enjoying Eggs Benedict and champagne, while Roxanne went hungry. She knew what those brunches were like, too — all-day affairs.

Rox could envision her mother now, in a simple but elegant summer dress, her chin-length white-blonde hair gleaming in the sun, sipping champagne in a garden behind some fabulous Georgetown mansion. She might be peering over her glass with her icy blue eyes, listening to some important senator talk about important issues.

Surrounding her would be lots of glamorous people, D.C. politicos, maybe some television personalities. Roxanne knew the types — she'd seen them here, in her very own home, on the frequent occasions when her mother entertained. It was about the only time her mother was ever home.

"The glamorous Washington D.C. hostess," the magazines called her. Too glamorous to care what her kids were eating for breakfast.

Rox's gaze moved on to the bulletin board hanging next to the calendar. There were the usual invitations, some engraved on fancy paper. None were for her, of course. One was from a senator and his wife, inviting Mrs. Easton to cocktails and dinner that same day. She's probably going straight there from brunch, Roxanne thought. She had a pretty good idea that she wouldn't be seeing her mother at all that day.

Rox wandered into the living room. The decor seemed appropriate for her mood — the dark woods and heavy brocades gave it a generally gloomy look. No one had pulled back the draperies, but Rox could imagine what it was like outside: sunny and warm, a perfect day for the beach. The crowd was probably already there, running and laughing in the sun.

Why hadn't Vince called? Of course, he hadn't exactly said he would. But Rox assumed that after their conversation he wouldn't be able to stop thinking about her. And that should have driven him to the phone.

He was definitely attracted to her. She could see it in his eyes. Boys were always attracted when they first met her. Wistfully she remembered those first few days at Kennedy High, when she'd had every boy in school eating out of her hand.

She'd certainly turned on the charm for Vince. And after all that talk about the beach, she thought she'd made it pretty clear that she wouldn't want to go by herself. Maybe he was even denser than she thought.

Her thoughts were rudely disrupted by a sudden, ear-splitting burst of heavy metal music. Rox stormed out of the room and down the hall to her brother's bedroom. Standing at the entrance, she glared at him and screamed in order to be heard over the stereo.

"Turn that thing down!"

Torrey grinned mockingly at her. "It's supposed to be loud," he shot back, making no effort to adjust it.

Rox spotted some headphones lying on the floor. She picked them up and threw them at him. "Use these!"

"Can't," Torrey replied. "They're broken. Mom was supposed to leave me money today to get some new ones, but she forgot. You're just going to have to suffer."

Rox was too weary to argue. She slammed his door shut, went back to her own bedroom, and shut that door, too. It helped a little, although she could still hear the pounding of the bass. It gave her a vicious headache.

What was Vince doing right that minute, she wondered irritably. Probably getting an earful from Jonathan, all about how Rox had manipulated him and what a user she was. All that junk.

She should be there right now protecting herself, making her moves.

Restlessly she wandered around the room, pausing to turn on the small television that sat on her bureau. She threw herself down on her bed and tried to watch.

It was a rerun of one of those dumb happy-family shows, the kind that was supposed to be heart-warming. Some little girl was crying, and a woman — her mother probably — had an arm around her.

"Now darling, don't cry," the woman was saying. *"It will be all right, I promise. You know, Daddy and I love you very much. We'll never let anything bad happen to you."*

Rox stared at the small screen and rolled her eyes. Those stupid shows! All those people taking care of each other . . . well, no one was going to take care of her. She had to make things work all by herself, and that was it.

Abruptly, she jumped up and turned off the television. She had to get out of this house before she went nuts. But where was she going to go?

Sitting down at her dressing table, Rox stared at herself in the mirror. She knew she was pretty enough to get anything she wanted. Surely that included making someone like Vince fall in love with her.

But maybe it wasn't going to be as easy as she had expected. He was so slow, so careful. He needed encouragement. She had to spend time with him, flirt with him, play up to his ego. Otherwise she'd never get anywhere with him. Suddenly she made a decision.

She got up and searched through her drawers for her bathing suit. The sleek white one-piece with its high-cut leg set off her tan to perfection. Rox took a moment to admire her perfect long-legged figure in the mirror. She was feeling better already. She imagined herself standing next to someone like that shrimpy Molly Ramirez, and the mental picture made her smile. After brushing her long hair, she applied a little mascara and just a touch of gloss to her lips. Vince was the type who probably liked his women as natural-looking as possible, so heavy liner and shadow were out.

Too bad she had to put shorts on, she thought. But she couldn't very well ride the bus in her bathing suit. The thought of the bus ride dampened Roxanne's spirits. That long trip on that hot, crowded bus — she'd be wilted by the time she got to the beach. And that certainly wasn't how she wanted Vince to see her.

But how else could she get there, she wondered as she tossed some things in a beach bag. Then a thought struck her. The enormity of her idea made her freeze with a bottle of suntan lotion in her hand.

Someone had picked up her mother that morning. She vaguely remembered hearing the doorbell ring while she was still in bed. That meant her mother's brand-new Mercedes was in the garage.

She sat down on her bed and thought for a moment. No one was supposed to touch this car. Roxanne couldn't drive it anyway. She could only drive an automatic, and the Mercedes had a manual shift.

Torrey knew how to use a stick, but he didn't have a real driver's license. He'd turn sixteen in eleven days, but right now all he had was a learner's permit.

Well, so what? A person didn't get arrested and thrown in jail for being eleven days short of a license.

She jumped up and ran back to the kitchen. Mrs. Easton carried her car keys in her purse, but Rox knew there was a spare set somewhere. She searched all over, fumbling through all the drawers.

In her determination, she tried not to actually think about what she was doing. This wasn't like her. She was always so careful . . . her mother might be neglectful, but that neglect meant a lot of freedom for Roxanne, and normally she wouldn't do anything to risk that.

But extraordinary circumstances called for extraordinary measures. Frustrated by her futile search of the kitchen, she ran to her mother's bedroom.

The maid didn't come in on weekends, so the room was a mess. Gingerly Rox stepped around bits of clothing and shoes on the floor, and examined the surfaces of every bit of furniture. Keys, keys, where would her mother keep the keys?

She opened a small drawer on the little nightstand by her mother's huge bed. Under some pieces of paper a bit of glittering metal caught her eye. Success!

She snatched up the keys, carefully closed the drawer, and hurried quickly to Torrey's room. She didn't bother to knock on the closed door.

"Here," she said to her brother, holding out the keys. "You're driving me to the beach."

Torrey's eyes gleamed. "In Mom's car?"

"You *do* know how to drive it." Rox's tone was flat. "You've taken it before."

Torrey stared at her suspiciously. "What makes you think that?"

"Cut the act," Rox said. "I've *seen* you. Last week, when Mom was out of town for two days, you were racing it on Oak Street."

At least Torrey had the sense to look a little nervous. "Oh, yeah?" he asked with false bravado. "I think maybe you need glasses."

Rox sighed. "Look, Torrey," she said patiently, "I'm not going to tell on you. I *could*, but I won't — *if* you'll drive me to the beach."

She couldn't believe what she was doing. She never thought she'd be encouraging her brother's wild behavior.

Torrey was surprised, too. She could tell from his expression. But he recovered soon enough.

"All right!" He snatched the keys from Roxanne's hand and started toward the door.

"Wait a sec," Rox yelled. She ran back to her room, grabbed up her beach bag and followed her brother down to the garage.

"Go slow," Rox warned Torrey as he fiddled with the garage door remote and set off the car alarm by mistake.

Torrey, for once, did as he was told. Carefully, he pulled the car out of the garage. Once they were in the street, however, he shifted into first, slammed on the gas, and peeled out, tires shrieking.

"Don't go so fast!" Rox screamed at him. "The last thing we need is some cop stopping us!"

The threat didn't seem to bother Torrey. "Calm down," he said easily, "I can handle it. And I'm doing you a favor, so I don't want to hear any backseat driving."

Rox watched nervously as he took a couple of turns much too sharply. And he appeared to have a maniac desire to pass every car in sight.

She switched on the radio, settled back, and tried to relax. She had some planning to do before she got to the beach. Obviously the crowd wasn't going to be too thrilled by her appearance. Somehow she had to get Vince alone. . . . She closed her eyes and tried to concentrate.

In her mind, she played out two or three possible scenes. She tried to anticipate every possible problem and figure out a way to deal with it.

Suddenly, her eyes were jerked open by the squealing of the brakes. Horrified, she realized that Torrey had come within an inch of rear-ending the car in front of them at the light.

"Torrey!" she yelled.

Torrey grinned. "How was I supposed to know that jerk was going to stop for a yellow light?"

Rox groaned. "Do you mind? I'd really like to get there in one piece."

She sank back into her seat. Oh, if only Vince knew what she was going through for him! Taking her life in her hands by riding with this maniac brother of hers!

Of course, she wasn't actually doing this for Vince, she reminded herself. He was only a means to an end. The poor jerk was going to end up with a broken heart. Well, it served him right for not being more aggressive in pursuing her.

"There's the exit," Rox pointed out. She tried not to look as Torrey dived carelessly into the right lane.

At least Torrey's obsession with speed served a purpose. They made it to the beach in record time, at least half an hour sooner than if they'd taken the bus.

They drove along the beach highway, and Roxanne searched for a parking lot that didn't look like it was overflowing. "There's a place to park just beyond that hot dog stand," she pointed out to him.

"No way I'm parking," Torrey said. "You think I'm going to waste a day at the beach when I've got this car?"

Rox looked at him nervously. "Where are you going? What are you going to do?"

"None of your business," Torrey replied. Without making a turn signal, he swerved over to the side of the road, in front of the hot dog stand. "Get out."

"You're going to have to pick me up, then. I don't want to be stranded here."

"Yeah, yeah," Torrey assured her. "I'll pick you up."

"At six o'clock," Rox said. "Torrey, are you listening to me? I said six o'clock."

"All right, I heard you," Torrey said in a bored voice. "Six o'clock."

"Right here, in front of the hot dog stand."

"Yeah, okay."

Rox eyed him worriedly. "You're not going to forget, are you?"

Torrey looked as if he were going to explode. "Six o'clock, in front of the hot dog stand! I got it! Now just get out of here!"

Rox opened the door but paused before she got out. Her voice softened as she spoke to her brother. "Torrey, please be careful, okay? Don't drive like a maniac."

Torrey raised his eyebrows. "Afraid I'll get a scratch on Mom's precious car?"

"It's not just that. . . ." Rox's voice drifted off. If anything happened to her brother, Roxanne would have to take the blame.

Torrey grinned at her mockingly. "Now don't you worry, big sister. I'll drive just like a little old lady. Will that make you happy?"

Rox sighed. It was no use. She got out of the car and shut the door. Immediately Torrey shifted, floored it, and sped off, leaving a cloud of sand in his wake.

Rox bit her lower lip and stared after him. He frightened her; he was so reckless. . . . Sometimes she wondered if he had even an ounce of sense in him. He didn't seem to care about anybody or anything. Sometimes she wondered if he even cared about himself.

Well, she couldn't worry about Torrey. She had her own problems to think about and herself to take care of. She slung her beach bag over her shoulder and started down toward the beach.

Chapter
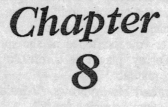

8

What a beautiful day, Katie thought. The water looked like a pool of melted sapphires, flecked with diamonds where the sun caught the waves. The sand was soft and warm under her feet. A light breeze tempered the sun's heat, and there wasn't a cloud in the sky.

It was as perfect a day as anyone could hope for, Katie decided. And here she was, surrounded by her favorite people in the world. The whole crowd had turned out for a day of sun and fun at the beach, and now they were tossing a Frisbee back and forth.

"Hey, Josh, catch!" Eric called as he flung the Frisbee. Josh made a dash for it, practically knocking Molly over in the process, but Stacy moved in neatly and managed to intercept it.

"No fair!" Josh yelled in mock outrage. He and Eric ran toward her, as if they were about to attack her. Quickly, Stacy tossed the Frisbee to Katie.

"Y'all are so good at this!" Charlotte DeVries exclaimed. "I just can't keep up with y'all. We didn't play much Frisbee in Alabama."

"You'll see plenty of it here," Katie told her, still holding on to the disc. "Hey, you guys, let's make this more interesting. How about dividing into teams? Girls against boys, okay?"

"Great idea!" Stacy squealed.

Katie grinned. She'd trained Stacy well. The younger girl was definitely getting into the spirit of competition.

Competition. It was the basis of so many of the arguments she'd had with Greg. He thought Katie was too competitive, too determined to win. Oh, the fights they used to have! But they always made up, Katie thought with a smile. Sometimes the making up almost made the fights worthwhile.

She looked at Greg now, across the beach, horsing around with Eric and Brian. Was there even a chance that he was feeling the way she was feeling? Sort of empty, sort of lost. . . .

No, she told herself firmly. It's over, forget him. Fiercely she did her best to shake off her sadness and turned to the others brightly.

"Ready to play?" she yelled. She waved the Frisbee in the air.

"Wait," Karen called. "How are we going to keep score?"

"Standard point system," Katie called back. "Whoever catches the Frisbee gets a point for their side. Ready?"

"Hold on," Brian yelled. "How come you get to go first?"

"Because I'm holding the Frisbee!" With that, she flung the disk out. She'd been holding it high, but she aimed it to drop, so it sailed out low. Molly darted out and grabbed it.

"One point for the girls," she called out.

Everyone was getting into the spirit by cheering and shouting support. Daniel intercepted Molly's throw and tossed it toward a group of boys. Matt and Jeremy both ran for it. Both of them were looking at the Frisbee instead of at each other, and they ended up smashing right into each other. In the end, Frankie got the Frisbee.

When Frankie tossed it, Josh caught it and held it suspended for a second. "Greg!" he shouted and tossed it.

But Greg missed Josh's call. He was listening to Charlotte, who was now looking up at him and smiling.

What a little flirt, Katie thought in amusement. It didn't bother her, though. Even though she only knew Charlotte slightly, she'd realized that Charlotte was the kind of girl who acted flirtatious around anything remotely male. Unlike someone like Roxanne, Charlotte never seemed to have ulterior motives. She was nice to everyone, and none of the girls seemed to mind the way she acted with the boys. She'll probably make a great student activities director, Katie decided. She was definitely social. Still, Katie couldn't help feeling funny at seeing Greg with *any* girl.

Of course, she knew she had absolutely no right to feel even the slightest twinge of jealousy. After all, it wasn't as if she and Greg were anything more than friends. He had every right to start seeing any girl he wanted to.

Thinking about Charlotte being the new student activities director made Katie realize for the first time that someone was missing. As the Frisbee sailed over her head, she turned to Lily, who was standing near her.

"Lily, where's Jonathan?"

Lily smiled, but it wasn't her usual smile. There was something sort of forced about it. "Um, I'm not sure. I think he had something he had to do."

Katie gazed at her curiously. It wasn't like Jonathan to miss a day at the beach with his friends. He loved this kind of get-together.

It also dawned on her that Lily didn't seem like herself. She was running around and yelling like the others, but not with her usual zany energy. It almost seemed like she was trying too hard to show she was having fun. Several times, Katie had noticed her staring off into space, as if she were worried.

Katie could tell something was wrong. After all, she was more than familiar with the signs of dejection.

Frankie made a wild fling of the Frisbee, and it sailed out into the water. Half a dozen kids went splashing in after it.

"I need a break," said a familiar voice behind Katie. "How about a walk?"

Katie turned and smiled at Greg. "Sounds

good to me," she said casually. But once again, her heart was pounding. Glancing back at the others, she saw that they were all running into the water. In unspoken agreement, she and Greg walked along the shoreline, away from the crowd. The laughter and yelling dwindled to a distant hum.

They walked silently for a few minutes. Katie could tell from Greg's expression that he didn't just want a break — he had something to tell her. Patiently, she waited for him to begin.

"I was talking to my parents the other night," Greg said after a while. "I told them about your college situation, how you turned down the scholarship at Maryland and how you want to study coaching instead."

"You did?" Puzzled, Katie wondered what he was leading up to.

"I told them you were going to go to Rose Hill Community College because it was too late to apply anywhere else."

"What did they say?" Katie asked.

"Well, my father thought it was too bad. Like you said, they don't even have a coaching program there. He also thinks you'll be bored out of your mind at Rose Hill."

"He's probably right," Katie said, sighing. "But I don't know what else I can do at this point."

"Dad had an idea," Greg continued. "He has this friend at the University of Florida. They're supposed to have a great phys. ed. and coaching program."

"I know," Katie said. "It's one of the best. But

the deadline for applications is way past. I'm sure the freshman class is already full."

"Probably," Greg agreed. "But Dad said if it's okay with you, he could call this friend of his and see if they could give you a late acceptance. I mean, maybe my dad could get you some kind of special consideration."

Katie stopped walking. "Are you serious?"

Greg nodded.

Katie didn't know what to say. She couldn't believe Greg had gone to so much trouble for her, that his father was willing to do this. Suddenly, she felt confused, overwhelmed with conflicting feelings. The University of Florida was the perfect place for her! But why was Greg doing this for her?

"I . . . I can't let your father do that," she murmured. "It's not right. I mean, it's like I'd be taking advantage of his position. Besides, I don't think I should be getting special consideration over other kids. It's really not fair."

"Was breaking your leg fair?" Greg countered. "I mean, it's not as if you planned for this to happen. You were all set to go to Maryland. Then you broke your leg and everything got messed up."

"And now I've got to make the best of it," Katie said shakily. "I have to take the consequences." Was Greg feeling guilty about what had happened?

"But breaking your leg wasn't your fault. Why should you have to keep suffering because of it? Is it fair for you to be wasting your time at Rose

Hill when you've got the potential to be a first-rate coach?"

Katie didn't trust herself to speak. Tears were stinging her eyes, and she was afraid if she opened her mouth she'd burst out crying.

"It's the perfect opportunity!" Greg said. "I know you really don't want to go to Rose Hill. This solves your whole problem!"

Katie started to speak, but just as she feared, what came out were sobs instead of words.

Greg put his arm tightly around her. "It's okay," he murmured. "Go ahead and cry all you want."

It almost felt like old times, having him so close to her. Finally Katie was able to speak. "It's just that . . . everything's been so awful, Greg. Every since that ski trip, it seems like everything's gone wrong for me."

"I know," Greg said softly. "I sort of feel the same way myself."

"Now something good has finally happened, and I'm so used to feeling bad that it's almost hard for me to let myself be happy."

"Go ahead and be happy," Greg whispered. "I wouldn't mind being happy, too."

Katie looked up at him through shining eyes. She realized then that they weren't just talking about college. They were talking about them, their relationship. And the possibility that they just might have another chance.

Suddenly she felt awkward and shy, as if they'd just met, as if they were on their first date. She smiled at him.

Greg smiled, too. It was a smile that held

promises, hope. For a magical moment they were silent, just smiling as they looked into each other's eyes.

Just then, a wave crashed onto the shore, splashing Katie's feet and she jumped. Her startled expression made Greg laugh. The spell was broken, but Katie had a feeling the magic was still there. Maybe they weren't ready yet to admit it to each other, but at least now she felt hope.

"So how about it?" Greg asked. "Should I tell my father to go ahead and call that guy?"

"Okay," Katie said. She laughed. "I'd have to be crazy not to take him up on that." She paused and her face grew serious. "I'd be grateful and proud to accept your father's help." Katie looked down and stared at the sand. "And, Greg?"

"Huh?"

"Thank you," she said simply.

Vince watched from a distance as the others caroused in the water. He'd been having a good time hanging out with them, but now he felt like he needed a few moments to himself, some time on his own. He really wasn't accustomed to being in big crowds. He decided to hike the nature trail above the beach and headed off in that direction.

It was nice to have friends, he thought as he walked the path with a determined stride. But it wasn't good to be too dependent on them. A guy had to be able to stand alone, to be strong without relying on others to support him. Vince had always prided himself on his ability to be on his own. He knew his interest in the outdoors wasn't one that a lot of other guys shared, but that had never bothered him. When he went out camping and exploring by himself, he could almost see himself as a wilderness man, strong and brave, standing alone against the elements.

Sometimes he thought it would be nice to have a girl with him, though. He liked the girls in the crowd, but it was hard to feel romantically interested in them. They were all so independent, so willing to take care of themselves. They didn't seem to need anybody.

Those were qualities he admired in a guy, but in a girl he looked for other things. He wanted someone who needed him, who would lean on him. A girl who was feminine and delicate, who would need Vince to be strong for her. Someone he could protect and defend. . . .

He thought about Roxanne. She was so beautiful, so desirable. It scared him a little. Could a girl like that ever be interested in a boy like him?

She had flaws, that he knew. But that didn't turn Vince off one bit. If anything, it made her more appealing. She was like a fair maiden who needed to be rescued. He thought about the way she'd cried that time, and his awkward attempts to comfort her. He remembered how she had looked at him, her pleading eyes. He hadn't done much to help her, but she still made him feel sort of like a hero. It was a nice feeling.

Roxanne . . . even her name was like something out of those tales of knights and dragons he had read as a child. He'd heard other kids call her "Rox," but that was no name for a graceful, feminine woman. The image of her face floated before his eyes. That long flowing red hair, that mysterious smile. . . .

Vince blinked. Was he seeing things? Had his imagination gone wild? Just ahead of him, emerging through the trees, was Roxanne!

She was no illusion, though, no figment of his imagination. Roxanne waved and ran daintily toward him.

"Vince," she murmured softly.

Vince gazed at her intently. "Roxanne, hi. I'm, uh, glad you came."

Roxanne lowered her eyelids demurely. "I wasn't going to. I was so afraid of facing everyone, afraid they'd laugh at me. But I knew you'd be here. And I knew you wouldn't let anything terrible happen to me."

Vince nodded. "But what are you doing out here on the nature trail? Why aren't you on the beach?"

Her smile was tremulous. For a moment, Vince thought of a shy, frightened deer.

"I guess I wasn't ready to face them yet. I needed to be alone." She raised her eyes and looked around her. "And I like it here. I love being out in the woods. It's so comforting."

What an extraordinary girl, Vince thought. "If you still want to be alone. . . ."

Roxanne lowered her head shyly. "No, not now. I'd rather be with you."

Together, they began walking along the trail. "There are so many trees," Roxanne murmured. "It's so beautiful here. Isn't that one over there pretty? It's sort of sad and romantic looking."

95

Vince nodded with pleasure. "That's called a weeping willow."

Roxanne's eyes widened. "Really? No wonder it makes me feel sad." She looked at him with such admiration that Vince felt like the wisest man on earth. "You seem to know so much about trees. I'll bet you could identify every one along this path."

"I'll try," Vincent said.

Roxanne thought she was going to die. How long was she going to have to listen to this — this nature lesson? And her ankle was itching like crazy. She'd probably caught poison ivy or something, scrambling through that dumb forest. When she'd seen Vince enter the trail, she'd had to take a shortcut off the path in order to get ahead of him so it would look like an accidental encounter. Now she had scratches on her arms from pushing aside branches, and her sandals were probably ruined.

And on top of all that, she had to listen to this *lecture.*

"Actually, there are three different kinds of maple trees in this part of Maryland," Vince was saying. "There's the red maple, the black maple, and the sugar maple. Now the oak tree here has a really interestingly shaped leaf. Look at this one."

Obediently Roxanne looked. "Yes, that's a very interesting tree."

"On your left, that's a sassafras," Vince continued. "I'll bet you didn't know that the bark can be used to make tea."

"No, I didn't know that. Amazing." Roxanne wondered how long this would go on. Miles of trees awaited them. With her luck, every one would have a different story.

"There are some chestnut trees over there," Vince said, pointing, "and that's another oak."

"Oh, yes, I've heard of those."

"Hey, I think I see a hickory over there!"

"Oh, wow." She had to change the subject. Roxanne smiled brightly. "You know, I read in the newspaper that you're a volunteer firefighter. I was really impressed. That must be awfully dangerous."

Vince smiled modestly. "I suppose it is. I don't really think about the danger, though. It's an important job, and somebody's got to do it."

Roxanne trembled fearfully. "But I'd be so scared. Have you ever actually had to go into a burning building?"

That question got him going. Vince started telling her a long story about some fire he fought. Roxanne actually found herself listening as he went on and on, talking about how the fire was caused by faulty wiring and how the people in the building suffered from smoke inhalation. It wasn't as boring as sassafras trees, at least. She didn't say much, but she encouraged him by giving him sidelong glances and nodding a lot.

"You know, Roxanne," he said, "firefighting is a team effort. But in another way, it's one man alone, against the odds."

"You must be very brave," she said softly.

His voice became low and intense. "At one fire, there was this kid, a small boy. He was so scared. His mother was prepared to sacrifice herself for him. She was so weak from the smoke she couldn't walk. She held the child out to me and begged me to take him." He paused.

"What did you do?" Roxanne asked. Despite herself, she was actually caught up in his story.

"I got them both out," Vince replied quietly. "I held the little boy with one arm and then I lifted the woman over my shoulder."

"Really?" Roxanne pictured Vince carrying the child and the woman out. She knew enough about Vince by now to realize he wasn't the type to exaggerate, or even try to present himself as more important than he was. She had to admit she was impressed — Vince might be a nerd, but he was brave. "You must be incredibly strong."

Vince shrugged modestly. "I work out every day."

Roxanne glanced at his arms. The muscles bulged below his T-shirt sleeve. "That's wonderful. I really admire people who take care of their bodies."

"You're really interested in my working out and stuff?" Vince asked. "I mean, I didn't think you'd care."

"Oh, but I do." Roxanne smiled sweetly. "Tell me more about being a firefighter."

"Well, another time I had to pull an unconscious man from a wrecked car," Vince said. "It was a four-car pile-up, right off the interstate. . . ."

This story wasn't as interesting as the other one. Roxanne listened for a while as Vince droned on and on in his boring voice. Now what could she do? Then she had an inspiration. She stopped walking and leaned against a tree, putting a hand delicately to her head.

"That s—sun," she said haltingly. "It's so hot. I feel . . . sort of dizzy." Then very gracefully, she crumpled to the ground.

It worked perfectly. Immediately Vince bent down and scooped her up in his arms. "Roxanne!"

Roxanne opened her eyes slowly. "Oh, Vince," she said weakly. "I must have fainted. I'm so embarrassed."

He was staring at her, his mouth slightly open. With satisfaction, she realized he was totally speechless. She gazed at him in the dreamiest way she could, hoping it was her beauty and not just the situation that made him look so stunned.

Kiss me, you idiot, she urged silently. When he made no move to do so, she decided to take matters into her own hands. She wrapped her arms around his neck, pulled herself closer, and tenderly planted a kiss on his lips.

When she opened her eyes, he was still staring at her, but in his eyes she saw exactly what she wanted to see. Vince was in love with her. There was no question about it. For the next few seconds, he seemed frozen.

"I'll take you back to the beach," he finally managed to say. Still carrying her, he started back down the trail.

"I can walk, Vince," Roxanne protested. "You can put me down." But Vince shook his head firmly.

I look ridiculous, Roxanne thought. This was not exactly the way she wanted to make her entrance in front of the crowd. On the other hand, she thought it might not be such a bad idea after all. She ought to get plenty of sympathy after Vince told them how she'd fainted.

But when they reached the beach, no one was there.

"Everyone must have gone home," Vince said. "Do you think you can stand up now?"

"Oh, yes," Roxanne said. As he gently put her down, Roxanne tried to mask her disappointment. This could have been her big day. She might have been able to make a real inroad into the crowd.

But she'd hooked Vince, and that was a significant accomplishment. With him by her side, the crowd would have to accept her. And the kids would be gathering here again. In fact, she'd overheard some kids talking about a beach party on graduation night.

The day's work wasn't over with yet. Vince was just standing there, looking uneasy and uncertain as to what he should do next. Once again, Roxanne took charge.

"Vince," she whispered, trying very hard to look bashful, "I really enjoyed myself today. Not the fainting," she added hastily, "but just being with you. I'd . . . I'd like to see you again sometime."

Vincent fumbled with his words. "Well, I was thinking, uh, yeah, well. . . . Do you think maybe you'd, uh, like to go out on a date?"

Roxanne cast her eyes downward. A date alone with Vince? Where would they go — to a greenhouse? Would she have to listen to another botany lecture to get an invitation to the beach party?

There must be some way to bypass that. Quickly she ran through her options.

"Vince, this is so embarrassing," Roxanne began. "I'm not sure if I should go out with you on a date. You see, I don't know if I would feel comfortable being alone with you." She looked away, as if she couldn't bring herself to face him. "I mean, after the way I acted out there on the trail. . . ." She let her voice drift away.

Vince actually seemed flattered. Roxanne felt reasonably sure he'd never heard that line before. He'd probably never been this close to a girl before — unless he was rescuing her from a burning building.

"Well, uh, maybe a party . . ." he mumbled.

"A party?"

"The crowd is planning a beach party for graduation night. Would you like to go with me?"

Roxanne pretended to consider it carefully. "All right," she said and gave him her best, full-force, knock-'em-dead smile. Then she leaned closer to him and kissed him lightly on the cheek. "It's a date."

Vince grinned nervously. "Um, it's getting late. Can I give you a ride home?"

"Oh, that would be wonderful," Roxanne purred. They started to walk toward the parking lot, but then Roxanne stopped. "I'm still feeling a little weak," she confessed. "May I take your arm?"

Vince looked pleased. "Of course." Clinging to him, Roxanne felt like she could have danced all the way to the lot. She was on her way!

Her heart sank when they passed the hot dog stand. She couldn't believe it! For once, Torrey had actually done what he was supposed to do. There he was, in the Mercedes, waiting for her. Roxanne looked the other way, hoping wildly that Torrey wouldn't see her.

No such luck. She heard the car's horn honking.

"I think that guy's trying to get your attention," Vince said.

Reluctantly Roxanne glanced briefly at the car. Torrey was waving to her.

"Do you know him?" Vince asked.

"I've never seen him before in my life," Roxanne replied smoothly. Keeping a firm grip on Vince's arm, she allowed him to lead her to his car.

Chapter
9

The cafeteria was in its usual noontime state of chaos. Students carrying trays and lunch bags zoomed up and down the aisles, waving and calling to friends. The air was filled with the buzz of many voices carrying on a hundred different conversations.

Lily was barely aware of the confusion surrounding her. Clutching her lunch bag with one hand and tugging at a lock of hair with the other, she stood motionless in the middle of the cafeteria. Her worried eyes scanned the large room for a sign of Jonathan.

But he was nowhere to be seen. Her anxiety deepened. It was now Monday, and she hadn't seen her boyfriend since he'd stormed out of the Senior Follies rehearsal on Thursday afternoon.

She'd called his house twice over the weekend, only to be told that he "wasn't available." What did that mean? she wondered. Was he out somewhere? Or was he just not available for *her*? Both times she'd left her name and requested that he return the call. So far, he hadn't.

That very morning, she'd arrived at school early and waited by his locker. He never showed up.

Lily was confused and concerned. Jonathan must be pretty angry at her. What else could account for his refusal to call her back? They'd seemed so happy together, she thought. She always seemed to make him laugh with her character impersonations. Then Lily remembered the fury on his face when he stormed out of the Little Theater, and she shuddered. Would he actually break up with her just because she'd urged him to write his essay? Would he really destroy a beautiful relationship over a little thing like that?

Not that the essay itself was a little thing. Without that essay, Jonathan wasn't going to graduate. The thought of that upset her almost as much as the thought of losing his love. Even if their relationship was over, even if he never wanted to see her again, she still loved him, and she couldn't bear the thought that he wasn't going to graduate. What would this do to his future, his college plans?

"Lily! Over here!"

She saw Frankie waving to her. Slowly Lily made her way to the table where Frankie was sitting with Josh and Vince.

"What's wrong?" Frankie asked as Lily sat down. "You look like it's the end of the world."

"It looks that way," Lily said melodramatically. "For Jonathan, at least."

"What are you talking about?" Josh asked.

Lily hadn't really talked to anyone about her fears. She felt funny bringing the situation up with Jonathan's other friends. It felt as if she'd be betraying a confidence. But sitting here with juniors, her classmates, she felt as though she could talk. And she felt the need to share her feelings with her friends.

"I'm so worried about him," she confessed. "He's been acting strange lately."

"How do you mean?" Frankie asked.

"He's been so moody. One minute he's horsing around and acting even crazier than usual. Then the next minute, he seems so depressed."

"That's odd," Frankie said, looking at her curiously. "Is he having problems with school?"

Lily nodded. "He skipped a French exam, and I don't think he's even made arrangements to make it up."

"You're kidding!" Josh said. "I always thought Jonathan was pretty conscientious about school stuff."

"That's not all, either," Lily continued. "He didn't turn in his final English essay. Mr. Barnes even came to the Senior Follies rehearsal to tell him that if he didn't turn it in by Tuesday, he wouldn't graduate."

"What did Jonathan say?" Frankie asked, her eyes wide.

Lily blinked rapidly to keep from bursting into tears. "Not much. He keeps acting like it's no big deal. And when I tried to say something about it, he got furious with me." She paused. "I haven't seen him since."

"Oh, Lily." There was a world of sympathy in Frankie's words.

"I don't know what to do," Lily said softly.

Vince, who had been listening silently, a perplexed expression on his face, finally spoke. "I don't see why you should have to do anything. It's Jonathan's responsibility to get his schoolwork done."

"But he hasn't done it," Lily said. "Something weird's going on. There's got to be a reason why he's acting this way, and I want to help him. But how can I help him if he won't even talk to me?"

"You said the paper has to be in Tuesday," Josh said. "That's tomorrow."

"I know," Lily said nervously.

Frankie leaned over and placed a comforting hand on Lily's. "You said you haven't talked to him since Thursday. Maybe he's written the essay and handed it in already."

"I don't think so," Lily said. "I saw Mr. Barnes this morning, and he asked me if I'd seen Jonathan. He looked worried. When I told him I hadn't, he shook his head and walked away. He didn't actually say Jonathan hadn't turned the paper in, but his expression made it pretty obvious."

"Maybe he's going to write it tonight," Josh suggested.

"Maybe," Lily said, but somehow she doubted it. Then she remembered something. "Uh-oh! Tonight's Senior Follies, and he's supposed to be there."

Just then, Diana Einerson stopped by their table. "Lily, do you know if Jonathan returned those overdue library books?"

Lily had forgotten about those. "I don't know."

"Well, I just saw a notice on the main bulletin board," Diana told her. "It said all school property must be returned by four o'clock today. That includes library books."

"What happens if he doesn't return them?" Vince asked.

Diana shook her head. "He doesn't graduate. Will you remind him, Lily?"

Lily nodded and Diana moved on. How was she going to remind Jonathan about anything if she couldn't even find him? "I don't even think he's here today," she told the others in despair. "What am I going to do?"

"Hey, guys, what's up?" Daniel plunked down on the seat next to Frankie. "Whoa, how come the long faces?"

Lily didn't feel like going into the whole story again, especially not with Daniel. Though they'd been friends all through high school, he wasn't one of her favorite people in the world lately.

Josh spoke up. "Jonathan's got some overdue library books in his locker. If they're not returned by four this afternoon, he won't graduate."

Daniel shrugged. "So tell him to return them."

"He's not here today," Frankie said.

Daniel thought for a moment. "We could return them for him."

107

"How?" Lily asked. "They're in his locker, and it's locked."

Daniel's face lit up. "We could break into it! I can do it. Those combinations are a cinch to crack."

"How do you know?" Lily asked suspiciously.

Daniel grinned. "Not how you think. See, when I first got here, I kept forgetting my combination. I figured out that if you press your ear against the dial, you can hear a little click when it hits the right number. Believe me, I've had to break into my own locker many times."

"Wait a minute," Vince said, his face stern. "Isn't this illegal or something? Wouldn't it be breaking and entering?"

It wasn't the legal aspect that was bothering Lily. She just didn't trust Daniel. After the way he had cunningly enlisted her to play a cruel prank on Karen, any plan he came up with was open to question as far as she was concerned.

Frankie and Josh knew what she was thinking. They'd been the ones who'd retrieved the fake interview from the Georgetown U. journalism department before it was read by the contest judges. They all exchanged glances.

Daniel must have read the doubt and distrust in their eyes. "Look," he said, fixing his eyes on Lily. "I know you don't trust me. And you've got good reason. That was a pretty stupid thing I did to you, and I'm really sorry."

He *sounded* sincere, Lily had to admit that.

"I really want to make up for it," Daniel went on. "I want to prove to everyone that I'm not such a bad guy."

Lily still had her doubts about Daniel's motives. Did he really want to help Jonathan? Or was he more interested in impressing Karen? If word got back to her that Daniel had changed, Karen would have to revise her opinion of him. Maybe then she'd make him editor of *The Red and the Gold*. Could that be his plan? Lily wondered.

But obviously he wasn't planning any tricks. He looked too sincere. And if he really could break into Jonathan's locker. . . .

"What if someone saw you?" Josh asked. "You could get into real trouble."

"I'm willing to risk that," Daniel said bravely. "I can do it after school. Everyone will have cleared out by three-thirty and we'll still have half an hour to get the books to the library."

Lily checked her wallet. "There are going to be fines. I've got five dollars. . . ."

Frankie looked in her knapsack. "I think I've got at least that much. If we pool our resources, I'm sure we'll be able to come up with the fine," she assured Lily. She looked questioningly at Josh, who nodded.

"I'm willing to chip in, too," he said. "How about you guys?"

"Oh, sure, absolutely," Daniel said quickly. "As long as it's not *too* much. . . ."

Vince was frowning. "I don't mind helping out," he said. "But to tell you the truth, I don't understand a guy like Jonathan. He gets himself in a fix, and then he expects his friends to bail him out."

"He didn't *ask* us to do this," Lily said impatiently. "We're doing this because we care.

That's all." She realized as she spoke that she had definitely decided to take Daniel up on his offer. She couldn't let Jonathan not graduate because of something as dumb as overdue library books. As for the essay, she could only hope he was taking care of that as they spoke. But she had an uneasy feeling that he wasn't.

"Okay, let's all meet at his locker at three-thirty," Josh said. "If there are as many books as Lily thinks, we'll need a few people to lug them to the library."

Frankie, Daniel, and Vince nodded in agreement.

"Okay," Lily said. It was the only way.

Lily's footsteps echoed eerily in the deserted hall as she walked quickly to Jonathan's locker. Josh and Frankie were already there. Daniel and Vince arrived a few seconds later.

Lily looked around uneasily. Except for the five of them, the hall looked empty. Even so, she felt like she should speak in a whisper.

"I feel sort of weird about this," she confessed. "Daniel, are you sure you know what you're doing?"

"Absolutely," Daniel said confidently. "There's nothing to it." Even so, he glanced around as if to make sure no one was watching him. "Why don't you guys sort of stand around me, just in case someone shows up. That way they won't see what I'm doing."

Lily and Frankie exchanged nervous looks. This definitely felt criminal. But they did as they were told, gathering closely around Daniel.

Daniel pressed his ear against the combination lock and slowly began turning the dial.

"I wish I could see Jonathan's face tomorrow when he opens his locker and finds all the library books gone." Josh said.

"Shhh!" Daniel ordered. "I can't hear the click if I don't have total silence."

There was total silence as Daniel continued his work. His face reflected his intense concentration as he spun the dial.

"Fifteen," he whispered. Then he turned the dial again, this time in the opposite direction.

"Forty-eight." He started turning it again, his brow wrinkling as he strained to hear the click.

"Thirty-two." This time there was a distinct click as Daniel pulled at the handle. The locker opened.

"Wow," Josh whispered in awe. "You could be a professional safecracker!"

"A noble ambition, to be sure," Daniel said wryly. He pretended to wipe sweat from his brow. "But I don't think I could handle it. Too much pressure."

Vince was shaking his head as he peered into the locker. "Holy cow! How could one person accumulate so many library books?"

"By checking them out and not returning them," Frankie said dryly. "It's easy."

Vince frowned at her. "It's not right," he said firmly. "Other students might have needed those books. It was very irresponsible of Jonathan to keep them for so long."

"Let's get this over with, all right?" Lily said briskly.

Daniel began pulling books out of the locker. *"Careers in Accounting,"* he read from one jacket. He passed it on to Josh. *"The Future of Electronics,"* he read from another. *"Research in Medicine."*

Daniel grabbed another stack of books and pulled them out. As he did, a pile of large note cards fell out and scattered all over the floor.

Lily bent down and picked them up.

"What are those?" Frankie asked.

Lily examined them, squinting to read Jonathan's squiggly handwriting. "They look like notes for a paper." She flipped through them, pausing to read. "Listen to this! 'There are so many options available to young people today, so many possibilities to choose from, so many roads to travel. We can be anything we want to be, and we can do anything we want to do. Graduation isn't an ending; it's a beginning. Personally, I see graduation as an invitation to take part in the real world, to explore life and discover who we really are and what we really want to do.'"

She paused and looked at the others excitedly. "It's his essay for Mr. Barnes! Look at all these notes. He's done all the work — it just needs to be typed up!" She scanned some of the other cards. "He's even got a title here: 'Ready for the World.'"

Josh looked puzzled. "I don't get it. It doesn't make any sense! If he's already done all the work, why hasn't he just typed it and handed it in?"

"I don't know," Lily answered honestly. "But look, there must be more than thirty cards here. It's got to be at least ten pages' worth of material.

Listen." She picked another card at random and began reading.

" 'High school is important, but, like most seniors, I've had enough of it. It's our last year, and seniors like me are ready to move on. We're all getting a little bored, and we're anxious to see what lies beyond Rose Hill. By this time next year, maybe even sooner, I'm sure that for most of us Kennedy High will just be a pleasant memory as we dive into the real challenge of college and adult life.' "

Lily stopped abruptly as she realized the significance of the words she was reading. Was that all she'd be to Jonathan in a year — a pleasant memory? Maybe this was why Jonathan didn't want to see her these past few days. He had been reevaluating his feelings for her. And it didn't look good. She was glad the hallway was dark. Her cheeks were burning, and she felt tears threatening behind her eyes.

Daniel took the cards from her and examined them. "Look at this, he's even got cards numbered to show what order they go in. Yeah, this is definitely an essay. He just needs to type it up."

"But it's due tomorrow," Frankie reminded them. "How is Jonathan going to type it up if the cards are sitting here in his locker?"

"I'll type it," Daniel said suddenly.

Lily's mouth fell open. "What?"

"I think I can read his handwriting," Daniel continued. "I'll take these home and type them up tonight. Then I'll put the finished essay in his locker tomorrow morning."

Lily felt suddenly guilty for all the suspicious

113

thoughts she'd had about him. "You'd do that for Jonathan?"

"Sure," Daniel said. Then he grinned. "Look, Lily, believe it or not, I actually *like* Jonathan. And I don't want to see him get in trouble. I know you guys think I only look out for myself, and sometimes that's true. But every now and then, I look out for other people, too."

Josh grinned. "It won't hurt your case with Karen, either. When she hears what a great guy you are, she's bound to see you in a more positive light."

Daniel looked slightly abashed. "Yeah, well, if that happens, it'll be frosting on the cake. Right now, I'm doing this for Jonathan." Then he laughed. "And if Karen makes me editor of the paper as a result, so much the better."

Well, at least he was honest, Lily thought.

"Wouldn't this be considered cheating?" Vince asked. "Like, having someone else write a paper for you?"

"But I wouldn't actually be writing it," Daniel said. He riffled through the cards. "He's got everything here. I'll just put the cards in order and type it up exactly as he's written it. It would be like paying someone to type a paper for you. It's perfectly legitimate. Only I'm doing it for free, as a favor." He beamed modestly.

Lily looked at Josh. "What do you think?"

"I don't have a problem with it," Josh said. "My typing's terrible, so sometimes I coax my mother to type my papers for me. As long as Daniel doesn't rewrite or anything."

Lily's eyes narrowed as she had a disturbing thought. Did Daniel have something up his sleeve? Was he planning to rewrite it, turn in something terrible, and make Jonathan get into *more* trouble? Could Daniel be trusted?

Once again, Daniel read her look. "Geez, Lily, trust me for once, okay? I'm not going to change anything Jonathan wrote, I swear. If you don't believe I'm sincere, at least give me credit for not being an idiot. I mean, do you think I want to get in any *more* trouble with you guys?"

Lily shrugged and Daniel grinned. "Look, I'll tell you what. Let's all meet here tomorrow morning, eight o'clock sharp, right here. You can all take a look at the paper before we put it in the locker. Okay?"

Finally, Lily grinned. "Okay. Thanks, Daniel."

"Don't mention it, he said grandly.

"It's weird. I still don't understand why Jonathan's been acting so strange," Josh said.

Lily's smile faded. "I don't know, either, and I'm really worried. I mean, getting this paper done for him might mean he'll graduate. But it's not going to solve his real problem — whatever it is."

Between the five of them, they were able to carry all the books. As they hurried to the school library, Lily tried to think optimistically. If all worked out as they'd planned, Jonathan would actually graduate.

But Lily was having a hard time feeling really good about it. After all, who wanted to end up being nothing more than a pleasant memory?

Chapter 10

Lily had trouble sleeping that night. Her imagination was working overtime, and the thoughts that ran through her head kept her from falling asleep. She couldn't stop dreaming up awful scenarios about Jonathan.

It was as if a drama were being played out in her mind: a play with several possible endings. In one scene, Jonathan found the paper in his locker. He immediately became furious with Lily for interfering with his life. He then threw the paper in her face and told her he never wanted to see her again.

In another scenario, he found the paper and turned it in. Everything worked out fine, he graduated with his class, and blithely headed off to college without so much as a kiss good-bye for Lily.

She wasn't sure which situation was worse. Finally, she fell into a troubled, restless sleep, only to find her dreams even more disturbing.

As a result, she overslept and had to dash around frantically to make it to school by eight o'clock.

Lily had hoped hardly anyone would be at school so early, but that wasn't the case. True, the majority of the students hadn't arrived yet, but there were still tons of kids scurrying through the halls, going to meetings or heading to the library for some last-minute work.

Lily hurried through the lobby. It was eight o'clock exactly. Daniel and the others were probably already waiting at Jonathan's locker. It wouldn't be right if Jonathan's own girlfriend wasn't there to share in the responsibility. Or maybe she should say *former* girlfriend.

"Hey, Lily!"

She paused reluctantly as Molly approached her.

"Where were you last night?"

Lily looked at her blankly. "Huh?"

"The Senior Follies! I thought you'd be there. Especially after the way you helped us on it."

Lily managed a smile, her eyes drifting to the clock on the wall. It was a minute after eight.

"Oh, yeah," she said quickly. "Well, I figured it's really just a senior thing."

Molly smiled warmly. "We would have made an exception for you."

"How did it go, anyway?" Lily asked.

"Great! We had a blast! And the audience was roaring. We messed up our lines about a million times, but nobody cared."

Lily was anxious to leave, but there was one

thing she had to ask. "Molly, was Jonathan there? Did he say anything about his essay?"

Molly looked confused. "Essay?"

"You know, the one for Mr. Barnes. Remember, he came by the rehearsal and told Jonathan he had to have it in today."

"Oh yeah, I remember. No, he didn't say anything about it. We were all getting so silly, I didn't even think to ask him. I'm sure he turned it in, though."

"Right," Lily said hurriedly. "Thanks, I'll see you later." She raced to Jonathan's locker. As she turned the corner, she saw her friends standing there, waiting for her. For a few brief seconds, her heart filled with pleasure. It was so good to have friends who cared, who shared your problems. This was what being in a crowd was all about.

As she joined them, Daniel proudly exhibited a neatly typed essay, the pages held together by a paper clip. He offered it to Lily. "Want to check and make sure I didn't pull something over on Jonathan?"

Lily felt like she should just say something like, "No, I trust you," but she couldn't resist taking a look at it. The title was centered at the top in capital letters: READY FOR THE WORLD. Her eyes drifted down to the opening paragraph.

As seniors face the end of the school year, some may feel like they're not ready to leave Kennedy High. Maybe they're afraid of losing the security of a comfortable environment, leaving old friends, going off into strange and unfamiliar territory. Not me! I can't wait to march down that aisle, take that diploma, and start living! This is one guy who's ready for the world!

Enthusiasm practically leaped off the page. Lily flipped through the sheets, noting that practically every sentence ended with an exclamation point.

"Looks good," she murmured.

"I didn't change a word," Daniel announced. Then he amended that. "Okay, maybe a verb tense here and there, one or two prepositions, that sort of thing. But I figure that's editorial prerogative."

Lily grinned at him. "You really want that newspaper job, don't you?"

Daniel rolled his eyes. "You still think that's the only reason I did this? What do I have to do to convince you I'm really a good guy?"

Lily shook her head. "You've already done it." She gripped the essay tightly. "And I hope you do get the editorship. You deserve it." She made a mental note to tell Karen what Daniel had done.

"Come on, you guys," Josh said, looking around apprehensively. "There are people around. Let's get this thing in his locker before anyone asks us what we're doing."

"Does anyone remember the combination?" Daniel asked.

"Fifteen, forty-eight, thirty-two," Lily recited.

Daniel twirled the dial and opened the locker. It was practically empty now that the library books were gone. Lily placed the essay inside.

"What if Jonathan doesn't come by his locker today?" Frankie asked.

Lily hadn't thought about that. She supposed it was possible, though, especially since he'd been so irresponsible lately. "Maybe we should go look for him," she suggested. "We could wait outside his homeroom."

"I think we'd better split up and cover all the possibilities," Daniel said. "You stake out the homeroom. I'll go to the gym and check out the boys' locker room. He might be cleaning out his locker."

"I'll look in the Little Theater," Josh offered. "They might still be straightening up from Senior Follies last night. Frankie, why don't you look in the library?"

"Okay," Frankie agreed. "Somebody should stay here, too. Just in case he shows up."

"I'll do that," Vince volunteered.

Lily's affectionate gaze swept over them all. "You guys are really terrific," she said.

"That's what friends are for," Frankie replied. "I guess we should set a time to meet later and report."

"How about at the sub shop after school?" Josh suggested. They all agreed.

Daniel closed Jonathan's locker and leaned against it, a faraway look in his eyes. " 'How the juniors saved Jonathan Preston,' " he murmured. "What a story this would make — "

"Daniel!" Lily exclaimed.

"I'm kidding," Daniel said hastily. "All right, you guys, let's man our posts." And they all took off, leaving Vince to guard the locker.

* * *

Roxanne strolled down the hall slowly, aimlessly. She had time to kill before first period, but nothing to do. Her thoughts went back to her old school, Stevenson High. Back there, she'd never wandered the halls alone. She could always count on having a group of guys hanging around her.

Looking down the hall, she could see Frankie with Josh, Daniel, and Lily. They had their heads together and seemed to be whispering about something as they walked up the corridor. They passed by Roxanne without even noticing her.

Rox hated not being noticed. But she felt more than anger as the little group walked up. Loneliness welled up inside of her. Why must she be excluded like this?

Just a few months ago, Frankie had been her best friend. She'd been like a puppy dog Rox could order around as she pleased. Why had Frankie deserted her?

It was because of the crowd. The crowd had taken Frankie in and left Rox out. Now she was alone.

But not for long. She thought about the beach party Saturday night, and her spirits lifted. It was going to be a fresh start for her. Soon she'd be right smack in the center of things again. Vince would see to that. And once Rox had some clout, once she had everyone's attention — boy, would she make them pay for the way they'd treated her. They were going to suffer as much as she'd suffered.

And there he was now, her key to a brand-new beginning at Kennedy High. She saw Vince standing there, in front of the lockers, staring into space.

Quickly she readjusted her expression. Time for the fair-madien routine, Rox thought wryly. With a sweet, shy smile firmly in place, she approached him. She noted with satisfaction that his face lit up the minute he saw her.

"Roxanne," he said in an almost reverent tone. He looked at her appreciatively. "You look really beautiful today."

Roxanne had a feeling he'd say that if she were wearing burlap. Luckily she had dressed that day in the hope that she might run into him. She was wearing an ultrafeminine sundress, a flowered print, with puffy sleeves. She thought it gave her a Scarlett O'Hara look.

"Thank you, Vince," she said softly. "Are you waiting for someone?"

Vince nodded. "Jonathan."

The name struck a nerve, and it took every ounce of Roxanne's composure to keep the sweet smile on her face. "Oh? I didn't realize you and Jonathan were good friends."

"We're not really. Actually, I barely know him. I'm sort of doing Lily a favor."

"A favor?"

"Yeah, she wants Jonathan to know about something she put in his locker. So I'm supposed to wait here in case he comes by."

"That's awfully nice of you," Rox said. "You really are a thoughtful person."

Vince blushed slightly. "Well, Lily's pretty anxious about this."

Rox made sure to look concerned. "It must be something awfully important."

"Sort of," Vince admitted. "See, Jonathan had this paper due for Mr. Barnes's English class. And if he doesn't turn it in today, he won't graduate."

Roxanne hoped she looked properly dismayed. "How awful!"

"Anyway," Vince continued, "Lily found these notes for the essay in his locker. She gave them to Daniel and he typed the notes up. We have to tell Jonathan the essay's in his locker so he can turn it in to Mr. Barnes today."

"I see," Rox said thoughtfully. "What's the essay about?"

"Something about what it feels like to graduate and go out into the real world. It's called 'Ready for the World.'"

" 'Ready for the World,' " Rox repeated. "That's a catchy title." She paused. "And you say Daniel wrote the paper for Jonathan?"

"Not exactly," Vince replied. "Daniel just typed up Jonathan's notes." Roxanne barely heard him. Her mind was working at full speed, and her thoughts were spinning. Jonathan. Daniel. Ready for the World. Mr. Barnes. She began putting the pieces of a plan together. . . .

"Roxanne?"

"Huh?"

"I was just saying that I'm really looking forward to the beach party after graduation."

Rox put her thoughts on hold and turned the full force of her charm on him. "Oh, I am, too.

And not just because of the party." Her voice dropped seductively. "I'd be happy going anywhere with you."

She raised her eyes to glance at the clock. There were only a few minutes left before the bell — and she had work to do. "I'll see you on Saturday, then."

"I'll pick you up at seven," Vince called as she turned away. She looked back and flashed him a slow, sexy smile over her shoulder. But as soon as she turned away from him, a different smile began to play on her lips.

Jonathan. He certainly never did anything to help her into the crowd, and now she had the opportunity to thank him in her own special way. Rox could never resist stirring things up a bit, anyway.

Confidently she set off for Mr. Barnes's classroom.

Chapter
11

The sub shop was more crowded than usual. It was the next to the last day of school, and a lot of students were getting an early start on their celebrations. The mood was very lively and exuberant, and Lily wished she could share those feelings. But all she could think about was Jonathan.

She finally spotted her friends gathered in a back booth and hurried over to join them. She didn't bother with any greetings, but instead got directly to the point.

"Did anyone see Jonathan today?" Her heart sank as Josh, Frankie, Vince, and Daniel all shook their heads.

"Me, neither," Lily said, and sank down into the booth.

"I waited at his locker till the bell rang," Vince told her. "He never showed up."

"I looked all over," Josh said.

"He has math class right after mine," Frankie added. "I hung around class for a while, thinking maybe I could catch him. But I didn't see him anywhere."

Lily buried her head in her hands. "I don't know what else we can do," she mumbled.

Daniel made an admirable attempt to sound cheerful. "Maybe he went by his locker between classes and found the essay."

Frankie, eyeing Lily with sympathy, picked up on his tone. "Yeah! Can you imagine his face when he saw that composition, all ready for him to hand over to Mr. Barnes? He's probably racking his brain right this minute, trying to figure out how it got there!"

Josh let out a false-sounding laugh. "Right. Maybe he thinks the elves did it."

Vince stared at him. "Elves?"

"Yeah! You know, as in *The Elves and the Shoemaker*."

Vince still looked puzzled and Josh explained. "You remember. The old fairy tale about the shoemaker who had all these shoes to make, and he fell asleep. Then little elves appeared and made the shoes for him."

"I don't know that story," Vince said politely. "I guess I didn't read fairy tales when I was a kid. I thought only girls read those kind of stories."

Frankie laughed. "Vince, you're such a chauvinist!" They all started teasing Vince, who took it all good-naturedly.

Despite their banter, Lily could tell they were all just as worried as she was. "I don't even know if Jonathan was at school today," she said. "Maybe he's so sure he's not going to graduate, he's not planning to even show up anymore."

"Like you said before, there's nothing more we can do," Frankie was saying. Suddenly Daniel jumped up from his seat and began waving frantically. For a second, Lily's heart almost stopped — could Jonathan have just walked in?

But when she turned, she saw it was only Karen coming toward their booth.

"Hi, guys," she greeted them cheerfully as Josh moved over to make room for her. "Hey, why the long faces? Just think, in only a couple of days, you'll have the right to call yourselves seniors!"

That notion didn't do much for Lily. "Karen, did you see Jonathan today?"

Karen paused. "Come to think of it, no. Why?"

Lily was about to tell her, when she heard Josh groan. "Oh, no. Here comes Mr. Barnes."

Lily twisted her head around and saw the English teacher standing over by the door, looking around the restaurant. When he spotted their table, he headed toward them with a decisive stride and a determined expression.

He didn't bother with greetings, either. "Have any of you seen Jonathan?" he asked abruptly.

"Wow, he's really popular today," Karen said lightly. She glanced at the others as she spoke and seemed puzzled by the generally tense expressions.

"No, we haven't," Josh answered for them.

Lily was almost afraid to ask the question that was uppermost in their minds, but the tension of not knowing was unbearable.

"Mr. Barnes, did — did Jonathan turn in his essay?"

"No." The teacher looked even more disturbed than he had at the rehearsal. "But I did find a rather strange note on my desk this morning."

"From Jonathan?" Lily asked hopefully.

"No. I don't know who it was from. It was an anonymous warning about an essay entitled 'Ready for the World.' According to the note, that essay was not written by the student whose name is on it, but by someone else."

Mr. Barnes didn't seem to notice the horrified glances that were exchanged at the table. He continued. "As of yet, I haven't received any essay by that title, and Jonathan's the only student who hasn't turned one in."

The point he was making was clear. Lily struggled for words. "What are you going to do?"

Mr. Barnes looked at her steadily. "If Jonathan doesn't turn his composition in sometime today, he's not going to graduate. And if I do find an essay from him in my office, I'm going to read it very carefully. If I have any reason to believe it's not his own work, I'll have time to notify the office and have his diploma withheld before the ceremony this weekend."

Lily bit her lip. Her mind raced frantically. She called forth every bit of her dramatic skills as she decided what to say. " 'Ready for the World,' " she mused. "That sounds so familiar. You know, I think that actually might be the title of Jonathan's essay. I could swear I heard him mention it to me, ages ago."

Mr. Barnes raised an eyebrow. "Really?"

Lily sighed and dropped the act. She looked at him pleadingly. "Mr. Barnes, Jonathan would never turn in someone else's work. That's just not the kind of thing he'd do."

The others were all nodding in agreement. "He's very honest," Karen said. "He wouldn't even consider doing something deceitful."

"He's got real integrity," Josh added.

"Really, Mr. Barnes," Lily said, "it's just not like him to cheat. I know him."

The teacher nodded slowly. "I know him, too, Lily. He's always been an excellent student. And I agree, it wouldn't be like him to turn in another student's work. I'd be very surprised if Jonathan had arranged to have someone else write his composition. I can't believe he'd jeopardize his future like that."

He sighed deeply. "I admire you kids for standing up for him like this. Jonathan obviously has a lot of good friends. But I'm afraid he's got an enemy, too."

Lily was looking pensive. "Mr. Barnes, could we please see the note?"

"I don't suppose there's any harm in that," Mr. Barnes replied. He reached into his pocket and pulled out a folded sheet of notebook paper. He handed it to Lily, who unfolded it and held it so they could all see it.

Warning to Mr. Barnes, it read. *If any senior turns in an essay entitled "Ready for the World," beware! It is not his own work.*

Lily handed the unsigned note back to Mr.

Barnes and shook her head in bewilderment. Who would do such an obnoxious thing? she wondered. Why would anyone want to hurt Jonathan? And who, besides their own little group, even knew about the essay?

Almost against her will, Lily's eyes turned to Daniel. But he looked just as shocked as the rest of them.

"Believe me," Mr. Barnes said, "I'm going to give Jonathan the benefit of the doubt. Like you, I don't think Jonathan would turn in someone else's work. But on the other hand, he hasn't been acting like himself lately. I'm not saying that I necessarily believe this note. But if I *do* receive a paper entitled 'Ready for the World,' well. . . ."

He didn't finish the sentence, and he didn't need to. The implication was obvious. He just shook his head resignedly. "Seniors," he muttered. "Who knows what goes on in those muddled heads?" With that, he turned and left.

For a few seconds the table was silent as they all contemplated what Mr. Barnes had said. Then Karen spoke.

"Will somebody please fill me in on what's going on?"

Lily explained everything in a tired voice. "Daniel typed the notes up, and put the essay in his locker this morning," she finished.

Karen looked at Daniel angrily. "Brilliant thinking once again, Daniel. Now you've gotten Jonathan in real trouble."

Daniel's mouth fell open. He was about to protest when Frankie spoke up.

"Wait, you guys, uh . . . I know who wrote the note. I recognize the handwriting."

Everyone stared at her. "Who?" they asked in unison.

Frankie sighed. "Roxanne."

Lily gasped. Roxanne! Of course! She had a real grudge against Jonathan. She'd jump at the chance to hurt *any* one of the crowd members.

Josh was shaking his head in puzzlement. "But how could she have known about the paper?"

Lily realized that Vince was gazing at them with an odd expression, a combination of perplexity and embarrassment. "I, um, I told her."

Everyone started talking at once. "You told her?" "Why?" "When?" "What did you do that for?"

"She came by Jonathan's locker this morning when I was waiting for him, and she wanted to know why I was standing there. I didn't see any harm in telling her."

"No harm!" Karen practically screamed. "Don't you know what that girl's like?"

Vince seemed surprised to hear such an emotional response. "Of course I know what she's like. She's a decent, warm-hearted person, who, incidentally, has been very lonely since she transferred here. I'm probably the only person at this school who's made any effort to get to know her."

Josh was looking at his friend as if he'd never seen him before. "Since when have you been such good friends with Roxanne Easton?" he demanded.

Vince smiled and his eyes went dreamy. "Since last weekend at the beach. I, uh, guess I sort of fell for her in a big way, if you know what I mean. In fact, I'm taking her to the beach party graduation night."

He was completely oblivious to the shocked expressions on the faces of his companions. "I never thought someone like Roxanne actually existed," he said seriously. "She's truly amazing."

"You can say that again," Frankie noted grimly.

Vince turned to her, an earnest look on his face. "Frankie, you must be mistaken about that note. Roxanne would never do anything like that. She's the sweetest, most innocent girl I've ever known. And besides, she wouldn't want to hurt Jonathan, or anyone else for that matter. All she wants is to be loved."

Daniel was shaking his head in amusement. "Boy, have you been taken for a ride!"

Vince stared at him in bewilderment. "What do you mean?"

Karen spoke to him gently. "Vince, you don't know the real Roxanne. Ever since she transferred here last January, she's been nothing but trouble. She tried to create a feud between the kids here and the transfers from Stevenson."

"She talked me into thinking all the Kennedy kids here were out to get us," Daniel said. "That's how she got me to use Lily to pull that fake interview stunt on Karen. I could kick myself every time I think about it."

Vince shook his head vigorously. "That's impossible. Roxanne wouldn't do anything like that. There's obviously been a misunderstanding."

"At the Valentine's Day Dance, she fixed it so

she'd have four dates," Josh told him. "She's always playing people against each other."

"She also tried to break up Holly and her boyfriend," Karen continued. "And she tried to steal Greg away from Katie. She even tried to give Katie a bad reputation."

"She was once my closest friend," Frankie added, with just a touch of bitterness. "But she did everything she could to belittle me."

"She uses people," Lily said firmly. "She's famous for it. She's a phony and a manipulator, and she's only nice to people if she wants something from them." Lily paused. Poor Vince. Did they really have to tell him *everything*? Yes, she decided. He had to find out before Roxanne could hurt him any more than she already had.

Vince didn't say anything. He just sat there with a stunned expression frozen on his face.

Josh put his hand on Vince's shoulder. "Sorry about this, old buddy," he said lightly, but his expression was sympathetic. "I had no idea you were getting involved with her, or I would have warned you. But it's better for you to hear this now, from us, instead of later — when she dumps you."

Vince didn't look stunned anymore. Now he looked devastated. "You mean, it was all an act?"

"She's a good actress when it suits her," Lily said.

"But . . . why me?" Vince said. "She seemed like she was really interested in me."

Josh shrugged. "Well, we don't really know what's happened between you and Roxanne, but we all know her track record. Roxanne's a user, and she must have known that you haven't been hanging out with us that long. Maybe she figured you wouldn't know about her."

Now Vince looked angry. "I didn't. I thought she was beautiful, sad, and lonely. She looked like she needed someone. Boy, do I feel like a fool."

"Don't take it too hard," Daniel said comfortingly. "A lot of other guys have been where you are now. Just ask Greg or Matt or Eric or — "

"Okay, okay," Vince interrupted him. "I don't need the details. I get the picture."

"Not to be really nosy or anything," Karen began, "but are you still planning to bring her to the beach party?"

"Are you kidding?" Vince slammed a fist on the table. "I may be a firefighter, but this sounds like one person who can never be saved."

Lily looked around the table. What a sad little group, she thought. Vince is crushed. Karen's angry with Daniel. Daniel's upset because Karen's angry at him. And I'm miserable over Jonathan. It's like a cloud of depression is hanging over this table.

"Well," Karen said, getting up, "I hate to break up the happy party, but I've got to get home."

"Karen, wait a second," Daniel said.

Karen looked at him suspiciously. "What do you want?"

"Listen, I didn't mean to get Jonathan into trouble, honestly I didn't. I'm really sorry about this. I only wanted to help, and that's the truth."

Lily jumped to his defense. Much as she'd doubted Daniel's motives in the past, she knew he had really knocked himself out for Jonathan. And now he'd gotten himself into more trouble, at least as far as Karen was concerned. She felt a surge of sympathy for him.

"He *is* telling the truth, Karen. We were all in on this, but Daniel did the real work. He just wanted to help Jonathan get out of this mess."

"Even if our plan didn't work," Frankie added, "it was a noble effort."

"Yeah," Josh chimed in. "I think Daniel here chalked up a few points this week."

Karen looked at Daniel evenly. Finally she relented. "Okay, I believe you. I guess I've underestimated you. Maybe you really aren't so bad after all." She actually smiled at him.

Daniel looked immensely relieved. "Thanks, Karen. Hearing you say that really means a lot to me." His face was expectant, and Lily could tell he was waiting for Karen to offer him the editorship of *The Red and the Gold* right then and there. But Karen merely smiled, waved at them all, and headed toward the door.

"Oh, well," Daniel said. "At least now there's hope."

Hope for you, maybe, Lily thought. But not for me. And not for Jonathan. She got up. "I'll see you guys tomorrow," she said.

As she made her way toward the door, she saw a pay phone on the wall. She stared at it for a moment, debating. She might as well give it one last shot. What did she have to lose?

She fumbled in her wallet for a quarter, put it in the phone and punched Jonthan's number.

It was busy. Her quarter came back. Impulsively, she put it in again and hit the "O" for the operator.

"Operator, may I help you?" came the tinny voice.

"Uh, yes, operator, I've been trying this number for over three hours, and it's been busy," Lily lied. "It's really important, and I was wondering if you could test the line for me, please?" She recited Jonathan's phone number.

"One moment, please."

Lily held her breath for what seemed like an eternity. Then the operator came back on the line.

"I'm sorry, there seems to be an unidentified problem with that line."

"Thank you," Lily said dully, then replaced the receiver. Well, that was that. There was no more she could do. Whatever happened to Jonathan would happen. He was on his own now.

Chapter
12

It was the last day of school. Funny, Lily thought, normally on the last day of school she'd be skipping or dancing all the way there. Instead, she was dragging her feet, and her backpack felt like it weighed a ton.

She heard a car honking behind her, but she didn't bother to turn around and look. Then a '57 Chevy pulled alongside her and she jumped. It was Big Pink, and Jonathan was behind the wheel.

Lily stood there, frozen, not knowing what to say. Jonathan had a funny, uneasy smile on his face, as if he wasn't sure how she'd react to seeing him. But it wasn't his expression that rendered her speechless. It was his attire. Instead of his usual fedora, Jonathan had on a mortarboard with a tassel. And he was wearing the crimson JFK graduation gown.

Lily finally found her voice. "Jonathan. What — what are you wearing?" It wasn't the most intelligent of questions. The outfit pretty much spoke for itself.

"I just picked it up," Jonathan replied. "I thought I'd see how it felt before I have to officially wear it this weekend."

Lily looked at him stupidly. "Then you *are* going to graduate."

"Yeah," he replied. "Can you believe it? I almost blew it. Barnes really meant it when he said I wouldn't graduate if I didn't turn in an essay. But I got it to him late last night." He pretended to wipe sweat from his brow. "It's a good thing I haven't turned the building keys over to Charlotte yet. I was able to get into the school, and I put the essay in his office."

Lily put a hand to her mouth, trying not to gasp out loud. "Jonathan," she said. "Did you *see* Mr. Barnes? Did you talk to him?"

Jonathan laughed. "Believe it or not, the teachers don't live at Kennedy High. And I don't think many of them are usually hanging around at eleven o'clock at night. So no, I didn't see Barnes. I slipped the essay under his door. But don't worry. He'll find it on the floor this morning."

Lily shook her head in dismay, but Jonathan was still prattling on as if he didn't have a care in the world. "So it looks like this boy is going to be marching down that graduation aisle after all."

Lily felt sick. He looked so relieved, so much like his old self. And now she was going to have to ruin it for him. "Oh, Jonathan," she said sadly. "Prepare yourself. You're in for a shock."

Jonathan stopped laughing. "What are you talking about?"

Lily leaned against the car and took a deep breath. "Mr. Barnes thinks that paper isn't your own work. He thinks someone else might have written it for you."

Jonathan's mouth fell open. "*What*? That's crazy! Why would Barnes think a thing like that?"

"Roxanne! She found out what Daniel did, and she sent an anonymous note to Barnes, warning him of a plagiarized essay. She mentioned the title of *your* paper. And Barnes told us if he got an essay with that title, he'd have to be suspicious."

Jonathan looked totally confused. "That's impossible! How could Roxanne know the title? I didn't even think of it myself until last night!"

Lily shook her head wearily. "Come on, Jonathan, we already know. We're the ones who arranged it all! It was going to work perfectly until Vince told Roxanne. You can't blame him, though. He really didn't mean to do anything wrong. He just didn't know what she's like."

Jonathan was scratching his head and looking at Lily as though she had just lost her mind. "For crying out loud, what does Vince have to do with this? Or Daniel? Or *you* for that matter? Lily, what's going on?"

Lily wanted to scream. Why was he playing this game with her? "Your essay! Barnes thinks you didn't write your own essay! Even though all Daniel did was type up the notes."

Now Jonathan looked as if maybe *he* was losing

his mind. "All right, wait a minute. Somehow we're getting crossed signals here. Lily, I wrote my own essay. I typed my own essay, too. Look!" He wiggled his fingers in the air. "I've got the blisters on my fingers to prove it!"

Lily was speechless. Jonathan sounded totally sincere. And now she was totally confused.

"Lily," Jonathan continued, his voice calmer now, "why don't you get in the car, and we can talk like human beings, instead of yelling at each other."

Feeling somewhat dazed, Lily did as she was told. She sank into the passenger seat. "Jonathan," she said, hearing in her own voice all the tension and strain of the past week. "Where have you been?"

"Listen," he said, "It's because of that essay that I haven't seen you all week. I've spent every minute working on it. I told my parents not to call me to the phone, and yesterday, when they weren't home, I even took it off the hook so I wouldn't be disturbed."

"I know," Lily said quietly. "I tried calling you. Several times."

Jonathan was silent for a moment. "I'm sorry. But I had to work some stuff out in my head. You know how crazy I've been acting lately!"

Lily nodded. "I knew something was bothering you. I hoped you would tell me about it."

"I couldn't talk about it," Jonathan said, "because I didn't even know myself. I mean, I knew I was feeling weird about something, but even I didn't really know what it was."

"Do you know now?"

140

"Yeah." He stared straight ahead and gripped the steering wheel. "Writing that dumb essay helped me figure it out. That's why it took me so long. I'd start off with one idea and make a bunch of notes. Then I'd realize it was all wrong, and I'd have to start again from scratch." He turned suddenly and faced her. "You remember what the topic of that composition was supposed to be?"

"Sure," Lily said. "Something about what it means to be graduating and going out into the real world. You said it was a really stupid topic."

"Yeah, well, I was wrong. It wasn't stupid at all. It was the reason I was acting so nuts."

Jonathan nodded slowly. He looked away, and again he was silent. Lily could tell from his face that he was trying to find the courage to tell her something.

Finally he turned back to her and smiled. "I started off trying to write a really upbeat essay, about how great it was to be graduating and getting out of here. I had all the notes down and everything, but I couldn't bring myself to type it up and turn it in. It was a big fake, Lily. It wasn't what I was feeling at all."

"You weren't happy about graduating?"

Jonathan's smile faded. "No, I wasn't happy. I was scared."

"Scared?" Lily found that hard to believe. She couldn't imagine Jonathan being scared of anything.

He nodded. "This isn't easy for me to say. . . . I guess I was afraid — of college, of the future, of going off into the unknown. I didn't want to leave Rose Hill." He paused, and his next words were soft but intense. "Most of all, I didn't want to leave you."

Through misty eyes, Lily gazed at him, and her heart melted. "Oh, Jonathan," she murmured.

He looked at her steadily. "Lily, I've fallen in love with you. I've never felt quite this way about any girl before. And I don't know how I can bear leaving you."

Lily wiped away a tear. "Jonathan, I was so scared. After you ran out of that rehearsal, I thought for sure you were furious at me. And when I didn't see you, and you didn't return my calls, I thought you never wanted to see me again."

"I've made your life pretty miserable this week, haven't I?" he asked quietly.

Lily debated, then decided she might as well tell the truth. "Well, yeah!"

"I'm so sorry." He banged his fist against the steering wheel. "I've been such a jerk! Here I was, totally miserable about the idea of leaving you, but at the same time I was doing everything possible to push you away from me!"

Lily put a hand on his arm. "It's okay. I think I understand now."

He sighed and looked at her with gray eyes that begged for forgiveness. "It's been so scary the past few weeks, Lily. I thought I was going nuts or something. I kept telling myself it was only the senior crazies. I thought I was really looking forward to graduating, but every time I thought about it, every time the subject came up,

I kept going into these panics and I didn't know why."

"Is that why you cut class?" Lily asked "Because you really didn't want to graduate?"

"Sort of. I mean, I want to graduate, but graduation means leaving. It means leaving Kennedy, leaving Rose Hill, leaving you. . . . I didn't want to leave; I *don't* want to leave. Does that make any sense?"

"So you figured that if you cut class, missed exams, and didn't turn in your essay, you'd fail, and then you wouldn't graduate. And you wouldn't have to leave."

"It's funny," Jonathan mused, "I really wasn't actually thinking that. But in the back of my mind, I guess that's what I was trying to do — to force the teachers to fail me. Then I could stay here with you." He grinned ruefully. "Of course, realistically, that's a crazy idea. And I knew that. That's why I never could admit to myself exactly what was bothering me. So instead of talking about it and trying to work it out, I just went a little crazy."

"You sure did," Lily agreed. "You had *me* really scared for a while there."

Jonathan looked at her nervously. "How do you feel now?"

"What do you mean?"

"Do you hate me for what I've put you through? Have I alienated you forever?"

Lily touched his cheek. Then she leaned forward and kissed him for a very long time. Jonathan wrapped his arms around her and held her

143

so tightly she could barely breathe. But Lily didn't care. Locked in his embrace, she felt like she was floating on a cloud of happiness.

Finally he released her. "Jonathan," she whispered, "I could never hate you. I understand, and I do forgive you."

"And?" he prompted.

"And I love you." She said those words with all her heart and soul. And she knew at that moment that nothing could come between them, that no matter what Jonathan did or where he went, she'd always feel that way about him.

Their hands touched, and for a few moments they just sat there, smiling at each other. She knew with total certainty that Jonathan felt the same way she did. Nothing could stop them now.

She hated to break the spell, but there was still something Lily wanted to know. "Jonathan, what was the title of your composition?"

" 'Mixed Feelings.' It pretty much summed up what I was going through."

Lily sighed in relief. "Not 'Ready for the World'?"

Jonathan looked at her, puzzled. "How did you know about that? That was the title of the first essay I wrote, the upbeat one."

"I know, I know," Lily said, grinning.

"Is that what all that business about Vince and Roxanne, and Daniel typing up my paper was about?"

Lily tried her best to explain. "We, that is, Daniel and Frankie and Josh and Vince and me, broke into your locker. We found the notes for the essay there."

"Wait a minute, back up," Jonathan interrupted. "Why did you break into my locker?"

"To get those overdue library books you had stashed in there."

Jonathan clapped a hand to his head. "The library books! Oh, no! I forgot all about them!"

"Don't worry, we returned them," Lily told him. "Which reminds me, you'd better start hocking your belongings — you owe us each a small fortune in overdue fines!"

Jonathan was gazing at her, a little shocked. "You guys did that for me? You're something else."

"That's just the beginning," Lily said. "Daniel took your notes and typed them up. Then we left the essay in your locker."

"How does Roxanne figure into this?"

Lily explained what had happened; how Roxanne had found out and written the note to Mr. Barnes.

"That definitely sounds like Roxanne," Jonathan muttered. "But why did Vince tell her about the plan? Didn't he realize she'd pull something like that?"

"Apparently not. It seems she's really sunk her claws into him. Now he has this major crush on her. Or *had*," she amended. "We set him straight when we found out. But you know, I felt kind of sorry for Vince. I think he was really crazy about her."

"So now Vince is a member of the VOR club," Jonathan said. "Poor guy."

"The VOR club?"

"Victims of Roxanne." He laughed and shook

his head. "I can't believe you guys did that! Knocking yourselves out to save my skin!"

"It's funny *now*," Lily argued. "But you had us really worried."

Jonathan stopped laughing. "I know. And I really feel honored that you guys would do all that for me. I'm lucky to have friends like that. And I'm going to make sure and tell them all on Saturday night."

"Saturday night?"

"The beach party, remember? You're still going with me, aren't you?" Suddenly his voice sounded anxious.

Lily smiled happily. "I'll go anywhere with you." Then she grew thoughtful. "But pretty soon you'll be going someplace I can't go. It's not going to be easy for me, either, Jonathan, when you go off to college."

"I know," he said. "It's like we've just discovered each other. And now we're going to be separated."

Lily reached up and pushed a lock of hair out of his eyes. "We don't have to think about that now. There's still a whole summer ahead of us. Let's think about that, instead of the fall. We've still got three whole, wonderful months together."

"And we're going to make the best of them," Jonathan added. "Let's make every moment count. Starting right this minute."

And once again he put his arms around her and pulled her close.

Chapter
13

"Hey, Rox! Get out of the bathroom, will ya? Or are you planning to take up permanent residence in there?" Torrey's aggravated voice came through the bathroom door loud and clear.

"I'll be out in a minute," Roxanne sang out. She sank back luxuriously in the tub full of bubbles. The warm orchid-scented water made her feel light and weightless. She couldn't remember the last time she'd felt so totally calm, so sure of herself, so full of glorious anticipation.

She supposed she should get out. It wouldn't do to look puckered. No, she had to look absolutely perfect tonight. Reluctantly she pulled herself out of the tub and wrapped her wet hair in a towel. Then she patted herself dry and finished off with orchid powder and lotion.

After slipping into her bathrobe, she opened the door.

"It's about time," Torrey growled, pushing

past her. "Ick! It smells like dead flowers in here," he added as he slammed the bathroom door shut. Roxanne blithely ignored him and strolled into the kitchen. She was in no rush. She had allowed herself plenty of time to leisurely prepare for this great night.

In the kitchen, she glanced at the calendar with mild curiosity to see where her mother was. Checking the date, she read that her mother was having dinner at a French restaurant, *Le* something-or-other. For once, she felt no resentment over her mother's absence. Whatever Jodi Easton was doing tonight, she couldn't possibly have a better time than Rox planned to have.

Roxanne poured some diet ginger ale into a champagne glass. This was a night to celebrate. After tonight, nothing would be the same. There would be no more loneliness, no more feeling excluded. Tonight Roxanne would make her grand entrance into the crowd.

She carried the glass back to her bedroom. Sitting at her vanity table, she picked up her blow dryer and started working on her hair. She worked slowly and carefully, brushing and blowing each long lock.

When she finished, she went to work on her makeup. Vince probably liked girls to have a natural, innocent look. On the other hand, how much longer would she really have to care what Vince liked? After tonight, she'd be on her way to acceptability. And who knew what might happen? She might not even have to leave with him.

She decided to go for a more dramatic look.

She applied a deep blue shadow, then carefully lined her lids. Mascara came next, then blush, then lipstick.

After that, it was time to get dressed. She'd gone over her clothes already, and her outfit was laid out on her bed. Rox had decided to wear light-colored clothes; it would be dark at the beach, and she wanted to be noticed. The pale beige pants hugged her figure and showed off her long legs, while her cropped white T-shirt just skimmed the top of her pants.

She slipped into her white sandals, and then selected small white pearls for her ears. There — she was ready. She looked in the full-length mirror inside the closet door and examined herself critically.

In all honesty, she had to admit that she'd never looked better. Vince doesn't deserve a date like this, she thought, smiling at her own arrogance. But she wasn't doing this for Vince. Tonight was her debut, and she looked absolutely ready for it.

She glanced at the clock on her nightstand. It was six forty-five — fifteen minutes until Vince arrived. She wandered out to the living room.

Torrey was slumped in an armchair, listlessly thumbing through a magazine. He glanced up as Roxanne entered, and showed only the smallest flicker of interest. "You going out?"

"Mmmhmm." She sat down gingerly on the edge of the couch, careful not to wrinkle her pants.

Torrey snickered. "Who's the poor sucker?"

"No one you know," Rox said airily. There was no way Torrey was going to get to her tonight. She felt too good.

Torrey shrugged. "I just like to know the names of the people I feel sorry for."

Roxanne smiled at him pityingly. "You know, Torrey, you should get out more. You need to find yourself a nice girl, get into a crowd, make some friends."

"Look who's talking," Torrey snorted. "You don't have a friend in the world."

Roxanne just continued smiling. Even a remark like that wasn't going to bother her. What Torrey said might be true now, but in a few hours. . . .

"What time's your victim coming?" he asked.

"Seven."

Torrey looked at the clock on the mantel. "It's almost seven now."

"Then he should be here any minute."

Torrey stood up. "I'm getting out of here. I'm not in the mood to see a lamb on its way to the slaughter."

A few seconds later, the strains of heavy metal rock wafted their way into the living room. Roxanne got up and surveyed the room. She plumped a few pillows on the couch. The pulsating beat from Torrey's room made her want to dance.

Would there be dancing tonight at the beach party? she wondered. She tried to picture Vince dancing, and laughed out loud as she imagined him moving awkwardly to the music. He wouldn't be the greatest partner in the world; she felt reasonably sure of that. But it didn't matter. Someone was sure to break in and rescue her.

Alone in the living room, visions of all the evening's possibilities floated in front of her eyes. Then something else caught her eye — the clock on the mantel. It was seven-fifteen. She frowned slightly. She had thought Vince was the type who would be extremely punctual.

Maybe he got lost, she thought. No, he'd brought her home from the beach last weekend. He knew where she lived.

She sat back down. Surely he'd be here any minute. She wondered if Jonathan would be at the beach party. Probably not. If her scheme had worked, if her note to Mr. Barnes had had an effect, he wouldn't have graduated today. She doubted that he'd feel like celebrating tonight.

She wished Vince would get there. It would take them a while to get to the beach, and she was ready to party. She grimaced as she thought about that long drive alone in a car with Vince. Oh, the price she was paying for acceptance into that crowd!

She looked at the clock again and almost gasped. It was seven forty-five! Where was he?

Now she was getting annoyed. How *dare* he be so late?

Feeling restless, she got up and went back to her bedroom. She gave her hair a few unnecessary strokes. Then she put on some perfume. She checked herself in the mirror. Maybe the blue eyeshadow was too strong for the outfit.

She used some eye makeup remover and set about doing her eyes over again in light brown. Yes, she thought, that was better. But this time as she examined her reflection, she wasn't smiling.

Dark premonitions began filling her mind. Fiercely she pushed them aside and went back out into the living room. She sat on the couch and stared at the door. Then, she forced herself to look at the clock. Eight-thirty.

A slow, dull realization crept over her. Vince wasn't coming. He was standing her up.

Hurt and humiliation churned inside her, and then flared up into a full-blown rage. She pummeled the couch with her fists. Vince would never live this down.

Karen wrapped her arms around her knees and curled her toes in the sand. The spectacular bonfire cast a glow over the beach.

Karen wasn't sure if it was the bonfire, the salt air, or being with her friends that made her feel so good all over. The cool summer breeze, the soft roar of the waves breaking on the shore, the stars twinkling in the deep blue sky, and the greatest bunch of kids in the world — it all added up to the perfect beach party.

Charlotte DeVries joined her. "This is such fun," the pretty blonde said happily. "I'm so glad I was invited."

"Has Jonathan given you the student events calendar yet?" Karen asked her.

"No," Charlotte replied. "But he's been much friendlier to me tonight. *Everyone's* been friendly! You know, I'm really starting to feel like this is home."

Karen knew what she meant. She was glad the crowd was taking Charlotte in. Having such terrific friends was bound to make a newcomer feel welcome.

Karen glanced around. The seniors were in high spirits as they described the day's ceremony to the juniors.

"Jeremy almost tripped when he was crossing the stage," Molly was telling them. "I thought he was going to fall flat on his face!"

"I almost did," Jeremy said, shaking his head in embarrassment and amusement. "And then I reached for the diploma with my right hand instead of my left. There I was, frantically trying to change hands, when my left hand got caught in my sleeve!"

"I forgot to switch my tassel to the other side when I was coming off the stage," Katie announced. "Do you think that means I'm not officially graduated?"

Stacy applauded. "Yea! Katie's going to stay."

Katie just laughed.

"How about all those speeches?" Greg chuckled. "I hope we seniors-to-be don't have to go through all of that next year."

All the seniors groaned in unison. "No kidding," Diana said. "Speech after speech after speech. I thought my ears were going to fall off."

"And they all said the same thing," Brian piped up. "If I heard one more person tell us about all the golden opportunities that await us — "

"And what about that congressman?" Holly interrupted. "A nice guy, but bo-ring!"

Jonathan jumped up and puffed out his chest in an exaggerated way. " 'Ladies and gentlemen,'" he intoned. "'They call this a graduation, and that signifies an ending. But they also call this a commencement, and that signifies a beginning.'"

A chorus of boos greeted his performance, and Jonathan laughed. "Okay, so I don't have a career in show biz." He flopped back down on the sand and draped an arm loosely around Lily. "Not like old Lil here."

Watching him, Karen smiled happily. It was so good to see Jonathan back to normal. And it looked as though all was well between him and Lily.

Jonathan planted a kiss on Lily's cheek and then jumped up again.

"Oh, no," Colin yelled. "Who are you going to impersonate now?"

"No impersonations," Jonathan replied, grinning. "This is me speaking now." He paused and looked around at his friends. There was no mistaking the affection that shone in his eyes. His face grew serious. "I owe you guys an apology and an explanation. And I also want to say thank you for putting up with me these past few weeks. I know I've been acting pretty weird. I've been feeling a little crazy lately about graduating and leaving Rose Hill and going out into the unknown. Maybe some of you have had some of the same fears I've had."

An abashed grin crossed his face. "If that's true, you've certainly been coping with it better than I have. Anyway, I'm truly sorry for all the problems I've created. I know you all have been worrying about me." He paused and looked meaningfully at Lily. She smiled at him, and silently mouthed, "It's okay."

Jonathan smiled back and then stared at the ground. His voice grew softer, as if the words he was saying were a little embarrassing. "Maybe I don't express myself really well. I mean, I know I have a tendency to act like nothing's serious and make a lot of jokes." He looked up and gazed at the crowd steadily. "Well, this is no joke. You people are the best friends a guy could have. I wish there was some way I could make up for all your worrying."

A silence fell over the group. Karen knew what they were all feeling — a lot of affection for Jonathan. At the same time, they weren't used to hearing Jonathan get serious like this.

"You still owe us, Preston!" Josh called out.

Jonathan looked at him seriously. "What?"

"Two bucks each for your library books!"

Everyone started laughing, including Jonathan. Josh's crack had lightened the mood.

"That was the next part of my speech," Jonathan replied. He reached into his back pocket and pulled out his wallet. Then, ceremoniously, he doled out money to Frankie, Josh, and Lily. When he reached Daniel, he paused.

"I want to thank *you* especially. How many other guys would break into a fellow's locker and type up an essay for him? Buddy, I've gotta say this — you've truly *earned* your place in this group!"

Everyone cheered, and Daniel beamed. Looking at Daniel thoughtfully, Karen found herself joining in the cheer. Daniel really was an okay guy. She could accept that now.

Jonathan still had two dollars in his hand. He looked around. "Where's Vince?"

"He's not coming," Josh said.

"Why not?" someone asked.

"Well, he's really down about Roxanne. I guess he just didn't feel up to a party."

Everyone groaned. By now they'd all heard the sad story of Vince and Roxanne.

"He'll get over it," Matt called out. "We all did! Roxanne's sort of like one of those twenty-four hour flus. You feel really miserable, but it doesn't last all that long."

"Yeah, I know," Josh said. "But he's pretty torn up. Wild as it sounds, he really had a thing for her. He thought she was the girl of his dreams."

"Look, can we please not waste valuable party time talking about Roxanne Easton?" Jonathan pleaded. "You're bringing me down. This is supposed to be a celebration, remember! And I haven't finished with my speech."

His face grew serious. "One thing I've realized over the past few weeks is that we've got some great friendships here. And we can't let going off to college put an end to that. I feel like we need to do something special tonight to show how we seniors feel about leaving you guys."

"Didn't the seniors have some sort of special ceremony last year at their party?" Brian asked.

"Yeah," Jonathan replied. "Phoebe and Chris and Woody and the rest of those guys each threw something of theirs into the bonfire to signify the

156

end of high school. But I had a better idea, and I passed the word to the seniors at graduation this afternoon."

"This is going to be good," Brian said to Karen.

Karen nodded. She was pleased about it, too. And she looked forward to playing her part in Jonathan's plan.

Jonathan continued. "We might be leaving, but it's not the end. We're just passing the torch on to you juniors and sophomores, so you can carry on. I thought we should each do something to signify that. And I'm going to go first."

He strolled over to where he'd left his backpack on the sand, opened it, and pulled out a large black book.

"This," he announced, "is the student events calendar, which belongs solely to the student activities director. I guess I've held onto it long enough. I hereby formally present it to Charlotte."

A round of applause went up from the crowd as Charlotte skipped over to Jonathan and accepted the calendar book. "Why, thank you, Jonathan," she crooned, cradling the book as if it were a bunch a flowers. "I'm just ecstatic to have this!"

Diana got up, holding a silver-plated compass in her hand. "As outgoing president of the Wilderness Club, I was going to give this to Vincent. But he's not here, so. . . ." She cupped her hands around her mouth like a megaphone. "Vince, wherever you are, carry on!"

Karen turned to Brian, who was sitting next to her. "It's your turn," she said, nudging him. Brian scrambled to his feet. In his hand, he held an old set of once-expensive Walkman head-phones. "As a symbol of WKND, I take great pride in handing these over to Josh. Keep those air waves humming, pal!" Josh accepted the head-phones amid another round of applause.

Katie went next. "I didn't think Stacy would appreciate an old leotard," she said. "And I couldn't drag a set of balance beams to the beach. So I brought this instead." The gold charm in her hand caught the light from the bonfire and twinkled. Stacy examined it in awe.

"It's for good luck," Katie told her. "Not that you need it. But when you go into those big championship meets, maybe this will remind you of our practice sessions."

The usually flippant Stacy was quiet and serious. "I'll never forget them. Or what you've done for me, Katie. But I'll wear this charm every time I'm in a competition. And I'll win them for both of us."

As the crowd cheered and applauded, Karen had a feeling they were all cheering as much for Katie and what she'd been forced to give up, as they were for Stacy and what she had to look forward to.

"I've got two things to pass on," Colin said as he rose. "First, for Greg, I've got this." He dangled the tassel from his graduation cap.

"Is this supposed to insure that I graduate next year?" Greg asked, taking the tassel.

"Nah, it's just a symbol of being a senior. And I figured the student body president had better remember what class he's in." Then he handed a card to Frankie.

"What's this?" Frankie asked, trying to read it by the light of the bonfire.

"It's my discount card for the computer store," Colin told her. "With the Computer Club's budget and the cost of floppy discs, you'll need it!"

"There's one more," Jonathan said.

"That's me," Karen said, pulling herself up. She looked at the newspaper in her hand, her last issue of *The Red and the Gold*. It wasn't easy giving this up. But at least now she felt like she was leaving it in good hands.

She'd prepared a little speech, and she took a deep breath. "As you all know, I've taken my time choosing a new editor," she said. "But this paper means a lot to me. Being the editor is a big job. There's a lot of responsibility involved, and the editor has to be up to it. But it's not just a question of journalism. I had to make sure the new editor would be someone trustworthy, someone who would take the job very seriously. I've thought and thought about this, and I've finally come to a decision. I'd like to hand my last issue to the new editor — Daniel Tackett."

And without any hesitation at all, she did.

The bonfire was dying down. Everyone was mellow now, a little tired from the day's excitement. A soft hum of voices filled the air as kids talked quietly with each other, reminiscing about the past year and discussing plans for the summer. Brian was leaning against a rock, his arm around Karen, and they seemed perfectly content to just stare at the ocean. Jonathan and Lily were huddled together, whispering, sharing private thoughts. Watching the couples, Katie felt a hollow longing.

She went over to Greg, who was lying on his back and staring up at the stars. He smiled when he saw her approach.

"Let's take a walk," she suggested.

Greg jumped to his feet, and silently they made their way along the beach.

"I had a call yesterday," she told him. "From the University of Florida."

"And?"

"They work fast there," she said. "I talked to this woman from the admissions office, and she said they've already spoken to Coach Muldoon, and to Mr. Romanski from the Fitness Center where I was working out."

"And I'll bet they had nothing but glowing things to say about you," Greg remarked.

Katie tried to sound modest, but she couldn't help a little pride from sneaking into her voice. "Yeah, I guess so. The woman said the university would be happy to have me as a student there this fall."

Greg let out a happy whoop. Then he grabbed Katie around the waist, lifted her off the ground, and swung her around. Katie was so startled she let out a little scream.

"That's fantastic!" Greg exclaimed, finally setting her down. "How come you didn't say anything back at the party?"

"I wanted you to be the first to know," Katie replied. She gazed up at him in the moonlight. "After all, it's because of you that I got in."

"No," Greg said. "Not because of me. Because

of you. It's your guts and your talent that got you in. You're an amazing person, Katie. Do you know that?"

Katie smiled slightly. "I know I've got an amazing friend."

In silence, they looked at each other steadily.

"Maybe," Greg said slowly, "more than a friend." It was a statement, but it was also a question. And now, finally, Katie knew the answer.

"Greg," she began softly, but that's as far as she got. Suddenly they were in each other's arms, clutching each other, holding each other so hard it was as if they were trying to make up for all the time apart.

"Katie . . . Katie, I love you," Greg whispered in her ear. "I never stopped loving you."

"I love you, too," Katie murmured. Her head was spinning. During all those lonely nights, this was what she'd wanted, this was what she'd dreamed of. And only her stupid pride had kept it from happening sooner. She wanted to laugh and cry and stay in Greg's arms forever.

"It's so crazy," Greg said, still holding her. "We finally realize how much we mean to each other, and now you'll be leaving Rose Hill."

"We don't have to think about that now," Katie replied. "At least we're together now. And that's better than having missed each other forever."

And as the waves broke against the shore, they kissed in the moonlight, trying to make up for all the lost time.

Chapter
14

Slowly Roxanne drew herself up on the couch. She was all cried out. She couldn't just lie there, weeping, giving up. She had to do something. She had to take action, get back in control. She was Roxanne Easton, and no one was going to keep her down for long.

She scrambled off the couch. Her thoughts were jumbled, her mind in total disarray. It was hard to think clearly. What was she going to do?

And then she knew. She had to confront Vince face to face. Talking on the phone wouldn't do. He had to see her, to really look at her and realize what he was giving up. Obviously someone had talked him out of going out with her. Now she had to stand up for herself. She'd managed to make him fall for her once. She could do it again.

She ran down the hall to her bedroom and checked her reflection in the mirror. Her face was a disaster, her eye makeup all but obliterated. Well, there was no time for extensive repairs. She grabbed a tissue, wiped off the streaked mascara and dashed across the hall to Torrey's room.

She didn't bother to knock. Yanking open the door, she confronted her brother, who was lying on his bed listening to his music and staring into space. Rox went directly to the stereo and lifted the needle.

"Hey!" Torrey yelled in outrage. "What do you think you're doing?"

"You have to drive me to the beach," Rox declared.

"Are you crazy? No way!"

"Torrey, please! It's important!"

He sneered at her. "Forget it. Or don't you remember the last time I took you to the beach? I came back to pick you up, just like you told me to. And you left me sitting there in the parking lot while you went off with some jerk."

"I'm sorry about that — " Rox began, but Torrey wouldn't let her finish.

"What do you think I am, your chauffeur or something? Like you can just give me orders and then dismiss me?"

"Torrey, listen to me," Rox pleaded. "Try to understand. This could be the most important night of my life. If you'll do this one thing for me, I promise I'll never ask you to drive me anywhere again. Please! I'm begging you."

She hated doing this. She hated having to beg and plead, and practically fall to her knees. But she'd do anything she had to to get to that beach.

163

Torrey just lay there, smugly shaking his head. Roxanne tried to think. Obviously, begging wasn't getting her anywhere. He was enjoying it too much. She had to try another tactic.

"I'll pay you," she said quickly. A flicker of interest appeared in Torrey's eyes. Encouraged, she tried to remember how much money she had in her wallet. "I'll give you twenty bucks to take me."

"Not enough," Torrey said flatly.

"It's all I've got! Look, I'll give you my allowance for . . . for the next three weeks."

"Hah!" Torrey snorted. "Payment in advance only, big sister. Fifty bucks right now, and you've got a deal."

"I don't have fifty bucks!"

"Then you ain't going to the beach."

Rox wanted to weep, but that wasn't going to help her cause. She had to get through to him.

Stony-faced, she glared at him. Her voice became low and threatening. "If you don't drive me to the beach, I'm going to tell Mother that you've been taking her car out. And she'll believe me."

Torrey didn't say anything, but his eyes widened. Aha, Rox thought. I've got him!

She pressed on. "Do you have any idea what will happen to you? You can forget about any allowance. And you'll probably be grounded for life."

Torrey stared at her for a minute. "Give me the twenty bucks."

Rox tore out of the room, got her purse, and returned, holding the bills out to him. Torrey was pulling on his shoes. He reached out and snatched the money from her hand.

"I'm not picking you up, you know," he growled.

"That's okay," Rox said quickly. Somehow she'd find another way home.

"And don't try to tell me how to drive," Torrey added. "If I have to take you to the beach, I'm going to at least have a little fun myself."

Roxanne eyed him suspiciously. What did that mean? Well, she'd better not ask. She didn't want to screw this up.

They went down to the garage and got the car. As Torrey maneuvered it out of the garage, Rox got a glimpse of his expression. Suddenly, she was nervous. She recognized that look. It meant trouble.

Sure enough, as soon as they reached the street, Torrey shifted gears, slammed on the accelerator, and sped out like a madman. He tore through the streets and raced around corners, narrowly missing parked cars.

Rox had to put a hand over her mouth to keep from screaming. She was terrified. "Torrey, please! Not so fast!"

He grinned devilishly. "I told you not to tell me how to drive!"

"What if the police see you!"

"Who cares?" was Torrey's blithe reply.

"But you're not even sixteen yet! You don't have a license! Torrey, if the cops catch you, you'll *never* get a license!"

Torrey's only response was to swerve into the

oncoming lane to pass a car that was way ahead of them. Rox looked at him in fear. He was enjoying this too much! It was as if he didn't care what happened to either one of them.

There was a curve coming up — a sharp one. Roxanne stared ahead in terror.

"Torrey! Slow down!"

But he didn't. Like a maniac, he took it much too fast. The Mercedes spun off the road and headed directly for the hillside. Roxanne covered her face and screamed.

Chapter
15

Roxanne opened her eyes. Carefully she moved her hands, her arms, her legs. She felt okay — tremendously shaken up, but nothing seemed to be broken. She turned and looked at her brother.

Torrey looked stunned, but unhurt. At least they were all right. A wave of relief passed over her, and then it was replaced by another emotion. Fury.

"Get out," she hissed at him. Torrey seemed to come out of his stupor and reached for the handle. He had to struggle with it to get the door open. And once Roxanne was outside, she could see why.

The car was a mess. She didn't think it was totaled, but the front was severely damaged. Roxanne didn't know much about cars, but even her inexperienced eyes told her the car was completely undrivable.

Torrey surveyed the car with a dismal expression. "Looks like you're not getting to the beach after all," he muttered.

"You idiot!" Roxanne screamed. "You moron, you imbecile! You could have killed us!" A car was passing by on the road. Frantically, she waved her arms in the air, but the car went on by.

"Don't blame me!" Torrey shot back. "It was your idea to take the car in the first place!"

"But you were the one who was driving like a maniac!" Roxanne waved wildly as more cars came down the road, but no one stopped to help them. "*Now* what are we going to do?"

As if in response to that question, a police car pulled up.

"Great," Rox muttered, shooting accusing looks at her brother. "I'm going to tell the cops *everything*. You're not going to get a driver's license till you're forty."

"Oh, yeah?" Torrey exclaimed. "Then you better depend on me making your life miserable forever."

A police officer walked rapidly toward them. "Are you kids all right?" he asked.

Torrey didn't say a word.

"Yeah," Rox said sullenly.

"A passerby saw you go off the road and called us," the officer continued. He walked around the Mercedes. "Looks like the car's in pretty bad shape."

Torrey remained silent, and Rox responded with another dull "Yeah."

"This your car?" the man asked.

"My mother's," Roxanne muttered.

"Who was driving?"

As Roxanne was explaining what had happened, another car pulled up, a green sedan with ROSE HILL VOLUNTEER RESCUE SQUAD printed on the door. A boy was getting out of the passenger side. The light from the street lamp shone on his face, and Roxanne gasped. It was Vince.

Roxanne thought rapidly. Luckily, her devious mind didn't fail her. If there was one thing she was grateful for, it was her talent for taking what life dealt her and making it work to her own advantage.

"I'm going to have to go call all of this in," the police officer said and walked back to his cruiser. Torrey swore and ran his hand through his short, dark hair. "Great!" he screamed, "I won't even be allowed to ride a *ten-speed* after this smooth move. And it's all *your fault!*"

"Torrey, cool it," Roxanne demanded, noticing Vince walking over toward the wrecked Mercedes. Suddenly, she burst into tears.

"It was all my fault," she sobbed, out of hearing distance from the police. "All my fault." Vince was now next to her, looking down into her teary face. "I was driving," she announced. "My brother jumped into the car, and he wouldn't leave because he was so worried about what I might do."

"What do you mean?" Vince asked, obviously very concerned.

"I don't know," Rox whimpered. "I had to get out of the house, I guess. I was so upset, I wanted to die. Maybe I even crashed the car on purpose."

"Roxanne! I — I'm so sorry," Vince said, his

voice trembling. "You could have killed yourself, and it would have been all my fault." He looked so devastated that Roxanne almost felt sorry for him. "I should never have listened to what they said. What do they know about you, anyway?"

He gripped her shoulders with his hands and looked into her eyes intently. "I don't care what other people think. I'll stand up for you, Roxanne. I'll fight them all for you! And I'll make them see you the way I see you!"

Roxanne threw herself in his arms. Vince kissed her fervently, with a passion that actually surprised her. Then she rested her head on his shoulder and allowed him to hold her tightly.

Over Vince's shoulder, she could see Torrey staring at her, wide-eyed and disbelieving. Roxanne threw him a brief, victorious grin. She'd had some momentary setbacks, but so what? As always, she'd risen above them. No one was going to keep her down for long.

Then she faked another couple of sobs on Vince's shoulder. It wasn't easy, though. She was feeling so completely, so deliciously successful. And that feeling alone was worth a wrecked Mercedes, the police . . . and the wrath of her mother.

Her face hidden in Vince's shoulder, she allowed herself another triumphant smile. Roxanne Easton was back in control.

Coming soon . . .
Couples #33
Mean To Me

"Hey, Zack the Hack!"

Zack felt his jaw clench involuntarily. He had to remind himself that this was just a dumb touch-football game on the beach. Zack could usually control his temper no matter what, but Stacy was really getting on his nerves. She had been on his case the entire time, making wisecracks every time he caught the ball or made a play.

"Hike!" Matt finally shouted, and Eric snapped him the ball. He dropped back and looked for an open receiver.

Everyone was going in all directions. Stacy ran straight across the goal line toward Zack, who backpedaled to keep up with her. Then she stopped dead and turned to face Matt.

"Here!" Stacy yelled. "I'm wide open!" Matt arched back and spiraled an easy pass over Daniel Tackett's head, straight toward Stacy's outstretched arms.

Something suddenly clicked in Zack's head. With a burst of speed, he dove through the air and engulfed Stacy with both arms, in a rugged tackle. The ball flew past the tips of her outstretched fingers, and they hit the ground together with a terrible thud.

Oh, no! Zack said to himself in anguish.

Slowly, Stacy opened her eyes and met his anxious gaze. Her wide-eyed, innocent look sent a flood of new sensations through Zack.

Suddenly he was accutely aware of the touch of her shoulder, how warm her skin felt against his own, her hair brushing like cornsilk across his neck, the intoxicating realization that she was wearing perfume.

"Are, uh, you all right?" Zack managed to stammer weakly.

"I'm fine," Stacy whispered, barely moving her lips. She seemed to be feeling the same tingly way he did.

Zack felt totally confused. Moments ago he'd been so angry and frustrated because of this mystifying girl in his arms. Now he wanted nothing more than to kiss her. He leaned forward and Stacy dreamily closed her eyes, waiting for the thrill of his lips on hers.